MY FAKE FIANCÉ

PIPER RAYNE

This book is a work of fiction. Names, characters, places and incidents either are products of the author's imagination or are used fictitiously. Any resemblance to actual events or locales or persons, living or dead, is entirely coincidental.

© 2022 by Piper Rayne

All rights reserved, including the right to reproduce this book or portions thereof in any form whatsoever.

Cover Design: By Hang Le

Cover Photo: Wander Aguiar Photography

1st Line Editor: Joy Editing

2nd Line Editor: My Brother's Editor

Proofreader: My Brother's Editor

About My Fake Fiancé

I never felt truly desired by a man—until him.

The second he stepped foot into my small town Alaskan inn, his gaze swept over my curvy figure with desire, igniting a flame I thought was dead. He flirted with me, and I might've left two chocolates on his pillow at turndown, but that's where it stayed.

Over the years, he's floated in and out of town while a friendship developed between us. It's probably for the best because I'm not a one-night stand kind of woman.

Which is funny because when he propositions me to be his fake fiancée in order to end a family feud, it turns out I *am* the kind of woman willing to pretend to be the one he's in love with.

my fake FIANCÉ

The Greenes

Hank's Kids
Cade Greene (35)
Co-owner Truth or Dare Brewery
Fisher Greene (33)
Sheriff
Xavier Greene (31)
Pro Football Player
Adam Greene (29)
Forest Ranger
Chevelle Greene (28)
Water Boat Tourist

Marla's Kids
Jed Greene (35)
Co-owner of Truth or Dare Brewery
Nikki Greene (32)
Radio Host
Mandi Greene (30)
Owner of SunBay Inn
Posey Greene (26)
Owner of Fringe

Hank and Marla's Kid
Rylan Greene (15)

Chapter One

Mandi

Running an inn in a small town in Alaska wasn't my dream. I fell into this profession because I'm the responsible Greene. The one who makes sure everyone's needs are taken care of. The practical one who saw a failing inn and thought it seemed like a sensible investment. It's not that I don't enjoy running the place; I do—most of the time. Then there are other times when it makes me question all the what-ifs. But I suppose everyone has what-ifs in their life, right?

Since starting a new marketing plan to bring in more guests—tourism in town is down—I feel as though all I do is check in happy couple after happy couple.

Like this latest couple in front of me who's fresh off their wedding day since they reserved the honeymoon package. I'm not disgruntled. I'm engaged myself. My new ring even sparkles as I accept the man's credit card.

"I love your ring." The woman peers over the edge of the counter. "It's shiny, which means it's new." She says it with the excitement one new bride feels when she meets another.

I glance down at the two-carat, pear-shaped diamond on a platinum band lined with smaller diamonds. "It is."

Although I also clean it every night. I'm trying to keep it looking as new as possible for when it's time to give it back.

"So, when is the big day?" she asks.

"Six weeks."

Her eyes widen. "Really? When did you get engaged?"

I hand over the guy's credit card and he wraps his arm around his wife. "Come on, honey. Let's leave her be."

He winks at me, but everyone knows a new bride wants to give *all* the advice. She's spent weeks, months, or maybe years listening to other people lecture her about what she should and shouldn't do. Now it's her time to shine in all her wisdom.

When she remains at the counter, I realize she's waiting for me to answer.

"About a week ago."

Her eyes bulge out as if they have Slinkys attached to them. "It took us two years to plan our wedding and it wasn't even half as fancy as most of our friends'."

I smile. "It'll just be family and close friends."

"Exactly what I would have wanted," the guy says, and she playfully swats his stomach.

"I have you in suite two thirteen. Top of the stairs and down the hall. If you need anything, please feel free to let us know. We want your stay at SunBay Inn to be everything you dreamed it would be." I hand over the keys with a welcoming smile to yet another happy couple who can't keep their hands off one another.

I can't fault the couples. I did a promotion focused on getting couples to stay here to gain some momentum heading into tourist season. Nothing says struggling business more than when you hardly see cars in the lot, people in the restaurant, or walking down the halls.

My phone dings from where I set it under the counter.

The couple glances back at me, but I smile, not reaching for my phone. I thought I'd put it on silent when I got in this morning. Every time I see someone's name pop up on my screen, I feel anxious because I still haven't found a way to tell anyone I'm engaged.

My phone dings for the second time.

The woman looks over her shoulder as she reaches the stairs.

I wave them off. "Come down for breakfast in the morning. The pancakes are fluffy and delicious."

She smiles just as my phone rings.

They're out of sight, so I snag my phone and hurriedly answer it.

"*Amanda Greene!*" my mom yells. "Please explain to me what I just got in the mail!"

"Seriously? Is it you who's been texting me too? I don't know what you got in the mail, but we've been over this. I'm at work. One text or phone call and I will return your—"

"You're getting married?"

The phone slips out of my grip, dropping to the floor, and the one time I wouldn't exactly mind if my phone broke, it lands screen side up with my mom's name still on the screen.

She's repeating my name like a mantra. "Mandi! Mandi!"

I bend down and pick up the phone. "What did you get in the mail?" A cold sweat breaks out across my body.

"Your wedding invitation. What do you think I got?"

"Oh." I don't know what else to say. My stomach twists.

"Oh? That's all you have to say?"

"The invites weren't supposed to go out for a few weeks."

"Mandi, that is hardly the point." She covers the receiver. Hank, my stepdad, must have come into the room and asked why she's screaming, because I overhear a muffled version of her telling him the entire story, including me dropping my phone.

"Mom?" I wait a few seconds. "Mom." She's still rambling to Hank. "*Mom!*"

"I'm coming down there."

"No!"

The chime on my door rings and another couple walks in, examining the small lobby area. They each smile at me. I put up my finger, giving them a "please be patient for a moment" smile.

"I have to go check in some guests. I'll be by after work to explain."

"Mandi, I am not going to wait until then. Hank and I are coming to the restaurant."

Click.

I stare at the phone. She hung up on me. Unbelievable.

After taking a deep breath, I regain my composure and turn my attention to the guests. This couple is just as cute as the last. She's petite with blonde hair, and he's tall with dark hair and light eyes. They're both dressed as if they're going to attend a polo match. Wheeling their matching luggage behind them, they approach the counter.

"Welcome to SunBay Inn," I say. "Checking in?"

The man gives me all the information I need while the woman wanders over to the display of brochures for different activities to do in the community.

"You have glass blowing in town?" she asks.

"Yes, and if you enjoy it, you picked the right weekend. Theo has an entire festival going on this weekend. There's pottery too."

The man glances at the woman as she blushes and says, "Like *Ghost*?"

He turns back to me. "She loves that movie."

"What's not to love?" I smile and accept his credit card.

Those small things always give me a pang of jealousy. The fact he knew she loves that movie, that it's a small inside joke between them because he knows her so well. When I think about being with someone, that's what I'm looking for. I'm not really interested in the big displays of affection like bouquets of flowers or expensive jewelry. Just someone who knows that the minute I walk into the house after a bad day, I just need a hug. Someone who orders my favorite takeout and surprises me with movie night at home on the couch. Someone who shows me how important I am in his life. I think it's the little things that add up day after day to make a big romance.

"Definitely make sure you take that brochure then. Theo, the owner, is a great host. You're sure to have a great time." I hand over their keys and direct them to their room.

The sound of tires screeching in the parking lot says my mom is here. The man stops at the window to look outside with concern.

"Excuse me." I quickly walk around the counter and out the door before anyone rushes in here, demanding answers in front of my guests.

But it's not my mom like I expected. It's the grandma gang—Ethel, Dori, and Midge.

They file out of Dori's Cadillac.

"Mandi, I know I'm technically your stepgrandmother, but the fact that Midge knew about this engagement for a whole week before me does not sit well," Ethel says from behind Midge.

Dori's evil glare suggests she's on Ethel's side.

I frown. "I'm sorry."

"Don't be. I can finally say congratulations." Midge takes me in her arms. I'm fairly sure my breasts are shoved in her face due to our height difference. "Welcome to the family."

Three more cars pull into the parking lot and my sisters and mom pile out of them, demanding answers.

I glance back at the inn. Sure enough, guests are peering out of the windows.

Guess I don't have to figure out how to tell everyone now. But I should probably start at the beginning and explain how I got myself into this situation.

Chapter Two

Mandi

Three years ago...

Rain pelts the windows of the reception area of the inn. I still have a handful of rooms available for the night, but I'm doubtful anyone will be passing through town at this time. Still, I have one reservation pending that I've been trying to stay open for. I called the number, but it went straight to a generic voice mailbox.

I finish the dusting, the last cleaning job I have to do for the night, and I look out the window. The town is quiet, as it usually is at this time of night. With the rain, everyone is probably inside.

A set of headlights shine through the window, and I pull away to keep from being seen, as if I'm this person's mother staying up waiting to make sure they made it home. I position myself behind the counter, pretending I'm doing something on the computer, when I'm really just playing my tenth game of solitaire. It's a ploy I use often so the guests don't feel the need to fill in the silence.

The chime on the door rings and the guest steps into the small area. I glance up and instantly force myself to look back down. This man is tall, though I can't see his face with his hood up. Trails of water run down his jacket, dripping onto the floor.

"I'm so happy you're still open. I was worried I wouldn't make it and my phone died." He holds up his cell phone.

"Good thing you made a reservation. As long as we have you down, we try to wait until you arrive."

He pushes the hood of his gray rain slicker off his head, and wow... this man is gorgeous. He has a beard that he keeps trimmed close, long hair pulled back in a ponytail, and even with the layers of clothes, it's clear he's muscled underneath. "You're like an angel after what I went through to get here."

I smile and pretend I'm just now getting him booked in when I actually did it an hour ago. "Did the bridge go out again?"

He shakes his head. "I came from the other way, but from what I heard on the scanner, the sheriff was going to go have a look at it."

"Are you a police officer?" If he worked with my stepbrother Fisher, I would know about this man.

He laughs, and it echoes through the stillness of the room. Sobering, he responds. "No, but I have to know what's going on in the area with what I do for a living, so I tend to listen just to make sure I'm not heading in a direction I shouldn't."

I type a few more fake keystrokes. "What is it you do? Do you want me to charge the credit card you have on file?"

"Please." He nods. "I'm a photographer for *National Geographic*. Technically, I'm just a photographer. They contract me for anything up in Alaska. But I travel all over for my work."

"That's an exciting job. Other than those crab fishermen

from the reality show, we don't get people who travel outside of Alaska very often." I slide his key over the counter, and he nods in thanks.

"It's not all great. At first when I was younger it was, but it can be lonely too. This last trip, I spent a month in a tent just to get the one shot I wanted."

"One shot?"

He shrugs his big shoulders. "See. Lonely."

"What do you do the whole time?"

He picks up his bag. "I take other pictures, but there's a lot of reading, sleeping. I can't even get a signal most times."

"Well, you're in room two oh six. Get a good night's sleep and come down for breakfast in the morning."

He looks around and bites his bottom lip. "Do you happen to have anything I could snack on?"

"You're hungry?"

He nods, but there's a pinkness on his cheeks that suggests he's embarrassed. "My mom would smack me across the back of the head for asking, but it was a long ride down here from up north. The rain slowed me down. I didn't want to stop because I was afraid you'd be closed by the time I arrived. I'll take some crackers or something. Whatever's easiest."

"Um..."

Usually, I'm very rule oriented. I don't open the kitchen for late guests because if the other guests get wind of it, they'll expect the same thing.

"Please," he says, putting his hands together in a prayer pose.

"Okay, why don't you go upstairs and get settled? I can cook something up for you quickly. Anything in particular you want?"

"Thanks." The relieved breath that leaves his mouth says he's appreciative. "Don't go to too much trouble. I'm an easy guy."

"Easy, huh?" One corner of my lips lift in a smirk.

His gaze fixates on my lips for a second and my body reacts as if he holds special powers over it, a zing of electricity racing through me from head to toe.

A sly grin crosses his lips. "Not that kind of easy, but it has been a long, celibate couple of months."

I smile. "Well, I'll feed you then."

He chuckles.

"A meal. I'll feed you a meal."

Again, his gaze runs over my body. I can't be the only one who feels this connection between us, right?

He steps back from the counter. "I'll go get settled."

I watch him walk up the stairs so quietly that I smile because he's being respectful of the other guests. It can't be easy for a body as big as his to move around quietly.

I step around the counter, walk over to the door, and put up the closed sign, then I lock the front door and turn off the lights in the reception area before heading to the kitchen.

Francois would hate that I'm in his kitchen. The last time I cooked pancakes for myself, he said I was never to enter his kitchen again. And he's not wrong. Although I'm the most responsible Greene when it comes to most things, cooking never really jived with me. My mom tried to have me help her when she had her salad dressing company, but I mixed up the french dressing and Italian dressing ingredients, causing her to have a lot of product she had to toss.

For family holidays, I always pick something I can buy, or sometimes Francois is nice enough to make me a dish to bring and share.

I should've paid more attention because now I have a hot guy asking for something to eat, and I have to come up with something. I never should've said the phrase "the way to a man's heart is through his stomach" is stupid—it's like the universe is giving me karmic payback.

"Thinking hard there?" His deep voice surprises me as I stand in front of the industrial fridge with both doors open, unsure what to take out. "Do you mind?"

He pushes off the doorframe and crosses the room in what feels like two strides due to his long legs.

"I can do it. I was just thinking what you might like."

He slides by me and our bodies brush. We both still for a moment and I suck in a breath. I haven't felt this kind of immediate attraction to a guy, ever. Maybe because I've known every guy in town for most of my life, but it's like this guy brought jumper cables with him and revived every nerve ending in my body.

"An omelet is easy." He smiles at me with some eggs in his hand.

"What would you like in it?"

After setting down the eggs, he returns to the fridge and takes out mushrooms, green peppers, and goat cheese. "I'm good with these. You take it easy. I can do this. In fact, if you want to head to bed..."

I raise both eyebrows. I might have an instant attraction to the man, but I'm not stupid enough to leave him alone in my kitchen.

He chuckles. "Is it odd that I feel like I already know you?"

"A little." I'm not going to tell him I feel the same way. "Small towns can do that to people."

"I'm Noah, by the way." He cracks an egg, so instead of a handshake, I get a wink that makes my lady bits go crazy.

"Mandi. Amanda."

"Which one do you prefer?" He takes a fork and whips the eggs.

I shrug. "Everyone calls me Mandi."

"Okay, Mandi it is."

I pull a pan from the hanging organizer and pass it to him.

He plops a pat of butter in it. "Are you hungry, Mandi?"

I shake my head. "No, I already ate dinner."

He exaggerates a glance at the clock on the wall. "It's way past dinner. Come on. I promise you'll love it."

The goat cheese doesn't look very appetizing, but I've never been a very picky eater.

"Don't answer, I'll make enough for both of us."

I lean along the counter and watch him chop the vegetables, crumble the cheese, and when his forearm tightens with the flip of the omelet, I'm worried that I'm drooling. Francois has never gotten me hot the way I am watching Noah right now.

"What would you like to drink?" I open the beverage fridge.

"Just a juice. Orange?"

I grab a bottle of orange juice and a water for myself. He plates the omelet, then puts the ingredients he didn't use back in the fridge.

"Forks?" He opens the wrong drawer, so I open the correct one and take out one fork since I don't plan on eating anything. He clears his throat and reaches past me to grab another one.

"You are a flirt, aren't you?" The question leaves my mouth and I feel heat rush into my cheeks. Did I actually just say that?

He stills and looks down at me. Down because he is

dreamy tall. "Only when I'm alone in a kitchen with a gorgeous woman."

My knees grow wobbly under his gaze. I open my mouth to respond, but nothing comes out.

He chuckles and moves past me into the dining room. I'm frozen for a moment. Never has anyone made me feel so wanton in such a short amount of time. For a second, I wonder if this is what Chevelle feels like all the time. Guys watch her cross a room when she's never even spoken a word to them.

I take a seat at the table across from him, and he forks off a piece of the omelet and holds the fork toward me. "Ladies first?"

I open and he slides the fork into my mouth. My lips cover the metal and bring the omelet into my mouth. He watches me the entire time I chew.

"It's really good." And I'm not lying. "The goat cheese brings a unique flavor that complements the egg."

He forks off a much bigger piece for himself. "You sound like you're a judge and I'm going up against Bobby Flay."

I laugh before taking a sip of my water. "I've just never heard of goat cheese in an omelet, that's all."

"Then I'm glad you'll always remember me when you hear goat cheese and omelet together. It's a trend that's on the rise, just wait and see."

I chuckle while he hands me the second fork. I'd prefer for him to feed me, but that's ludicrous since we're strangers.

We finish eating, chatting about Sunrise Bay. He's only here for the night because he has to catch a flight to go do another job.

"Where are you from?" I ask when we're finished, as I put the dishes in the sink.

"Little bit of everywhere. I have a small place in New

York City, but half the time I'm subletting it to my friends and colleagues."

I can't imagine what it would be like not being surrounded by family all the time. Sunrise Bay is not only my home, but my entire family lives here—except for my dad, but I don't much care about him.

We walk up the stairs and I stop at his room. He inserts his key and I glance in and see his suitcase on the chair in the corner.

"This is me," he says.

I chuckle since I'm the one who assigned him the room. "I'm down the hall in the employee room."

"Don't go sneaking into my room in the middle of the night, Mandi."

I laugh, unsure what to say.

"Thanks for a great night after a shitty day. I'll give you five stars on Yelp," he says.

"Thank you." I take a step down the hall. "Good night, Noah."

"Good night." He stands in the open doorway, watching me.

I walk to my room at the far end of the hall, the one whoever is working the overnight stays in. Opening the door, I glance over my shoulder and see him still staring at me.

"I have this sudden urge to listen to 'Mandy' by Barry Manilow now," he says.

I shake my head. "Rumor is that song is about a dog."

"Really? Well, that's disappointing. See you next time I'm up north."

I wave. "Bye, Noah."

I hurry into my room and shut the door before falling on

the bed. Did that actually happen? I'm not in some weird movie where this was all a dream, right?

I pull out a hair on my forearm. Ouch. Okay, Noah is very real. Even if he does seem like my dream man.

Chapter Three

Mandi

A few months later...

After a month and a half of scouring the reservations for Noah's name and taking the night shifts in case he happened to pop in one night, I gave up. I told myself that yeah, there might've been a connection, but I'm not looking for a one-night stand, and no matter how hot the man is, that's about all that's on the table with a man who travels the world.

So I'm surprised when after coming in today and putting my coat on the hook, I feel Trina's gaze on me. She's got the same creepy smile she had when she thought Adele had checked in—only for us to find out it was an impersonator who had been hired by a man whose wife loved her.

"What?" I ask as I type my password into the computer.

"You should check the restaurant." Trina's smile widens.

I narrow my eyes then head that way. "Tell me what happened? Did someone call Francois Frank again? I told my brothers to stop joking around with him. He's brilliant at what he does and..." I stop in my tracks when I spot Noah at one of the tables by the window.

He's sporting the ponytail, although with completely dry brown hair this time. His long-sleeve shirt is taut along the shoulders and biceps, the sleeves pushed up and revealing the corded forearms I admired the night we met.

"He's here," Trina whispers in my ear. Except Trina's idea of whispering is more like talking at a normal volume.

"What's up, girls? Baby is hungry." Nikki's voice comes from behind me.

When I turn, I find her and Posey.

"What are we staring at?" Posey looks over my shoulder. "The lumberjack guy?"

I shake my head. "No."

"Yes," Trina adds. "That's Noah. He's the guy who checked in three months ago and made Mandi orgasm over an omelet."

I really regret telling her all the details the morning after he checked out.

I push all three of them back into the reception area before he spots us.

"Hey, baby in the tummy," Nikki complains. "And I'm sorry, he's cute and all, but you can't marry him."

My forehead wrinkles. "Excuse me? No one said anything about marrying him."

"I wouldn't call him cute, Nik, more like hunk on a stick." Posey leans to the side to try to get another look at him.

"I just went over names with Logan last night and there's only one boy name we agree on."

"You've been holding out on me all morning?" Posey asks, easily distracted from Noah—for the record, I don't understand how he doesn't hold her attention.

"We both like Noah," Nikki says as though it's obvious. "I don't want some weird confusion if Mandi marries a Noah and my baby is named Noah. We'd always have to be, like, 'Mandi's Noah' or 'baby Noah' and what will that mean for my poor son when he brings home his first girlfriend and his family calls him 'baby Noah' all the time?"

We all stare at her for a moment.

"Getting a little ahead of ourselves," I say. "Plus, there's no future with him anyway. Last time he was here was three months ago."

Nikki leans back to look at him. "What does he do?"

"He's a photographer."

Nikki's face lights up. "Oh, I want to get pregnancy photos."

"Are you sure you want a guy named Noah photographing a Noah in your belly?" Posey asks and laughs.

Nikki, of course, doesn't find it funny. Pregnancy hormones have made her humorous side disappear.

"Can we eat?" Nikki whines, ignoring our sister.

The front desk bell rings and I silently plea for Trina to stay on shift a smidge longer so I can get my sisters handled. Understanding my family well enough, Trina sighs but goes to the desk to handle the guest.

I pick up two menus and seat my sisters as far away from Noah as I can, but the restaurant isn't that big.

"You're crazy." Posey picks up the menus from the table I took them to and walks toward Noah.

Nikki groans and follows. Posey positions them to the side of him, on the inside of the restaurant because they know my family doesn't get the primo spots by the windows.

"Please tell Frank to hurry, the baby is kicking because it's starving." Nikki rubs her belly.

"How does Logan handle you?" Posey asks, looking at our sister's belly in disgust.

"You just wait. One day you'll be complaining while your husband can just sit there next to you, eat whatever he wants without heartburn, not need help standing up, and not need anyone to tie his shoes." She sounds as if she's ready to cry, so I give Posey a look over Nikki's shoulder that says to cool it with her.

Posey picks up her menu. "Goat cheese omelet? When did you put this on the breakfast menu?"

I clear my throat. "A while ago."

So far, Noah is busy staring out the window while glancing at his phone every so often. He doesn't have a meal in front of him and I suppose I should really go say hello. What kind of innkeeper would I be if I didn't?

"Mandi, breakfast?" Nikki says.

"You're not her wicked stepsister," Posey says.

"That would be me!" Chevelle comes in wearing her running gear and sits down next to Posey while staring at Nikki's stomach. "Whoa, I think you grew five inches since yesterday. Ouch!" She looks at Posey and rubs her leg. Luckily, she seems to have understood the message. "But you're as radiant as always. You can't buy that natural glow."

Nikki shoots Chevelle a small smile, but I know deep down she's wishing us all horrible pregnancies.

"Check out the hunk," Posey says, eyeing Noah once more.

"Eh, I'm not much of a ponytail girl, but those muscles look like they could rip that shirt in half." Chevelle stacks the containers of jam, making a pyramid like she always does. Soon the creamer will be the second level.

"His name is Noah, and although Nikki's declared that Mandi can't marry him, I figure she can sleep with him and have some fun."

Chevelle repositions her blonde ponytail. "Why can't she marry him?"

"Because Nikki's naming her baby Noah, so I guess that

goes for all three of us," Posey says. "As if finding a man in our small town isn't hard enough, we need to scratch all Noahs off the list now."

Nikki looks at Posey as though she wants to fork out her eye.

"Let me go get you some coffee and muffins." I pat my sister's shoulder and head into the kitchen, thankfully without Noah spotting me.

"Damn it!" Rachel, one of the servers, screams and runs over to the faucet.

Francois rings the bell that an order is ready, and I spot a goat cheese omelet on the plate.

"Can you take Rachel's order? She burned her finger because even though I told her not to touch the pan, she did. I think we need to hire smarter people." Frank, a.k.a. Francois, rolls his eyes. He's never been happy with one person I've hired.

"Which table?" I ask.

"Five, and I have an order of pancakes for that table too. Hold up." He positions another plate beside the omelet.

"How are you, Rachel?" I call.

The sous-chef, Nadia, is next to her. She shakes her head. "Let me get some Neosporin and a Band-Aid for her. Then she'll be good."

"And by then my food is cold. I do not want a bad review, Amanda. If I get a bad review, I leave this place." Francois smacks his spatula on the grill.

"You threaten to leave every day." I pick up the dishes, knowing I have no chance of getting out of this. "I've got it."

I walk out of the kitchen and Nikki looks up with hopeful eyes, only to give me her worst death glare once she realizes I'm holding someone else's order.

I give her a look that says to give me a second, I'll get her food, and head to Noah's table. I go over about a million catchy, flirty things to say. Things that maybe he'll replay back to himself later tonight. But when I arrive at the table and he looks up and sees me, all that comes out is, "It's been a while."

He smiles and I want to knock myself unconscious with the plate.

I lower his food to the table. The exact omelet I watched him eat three months ago and a stack of pancakes. "I'll go grab some syrup."

"Why don't you have a seat? Like you said, it's been a while."

I bite the inside of my cheek. "I'm not sure why I said that. It's not like you owe me anything."

He laughs. "I kind of like that you missed me." He uses his boot to kick out the chair opposite him. "Sit."

"Mandi!" Nikki whisper-shouts my name as if she's on the edge of sanity.

"I have a really demanding pregnant guest. Give me a minute."

He nods. "Sure thing."

Nikki says my name again and I raise my finger, heading into the kitchen.

Luckily, Nadia has Rachel all fixed up. "Thanks, Mandi."

"You're welcome. I need some muffins and fruit for Nikki out there."

"Put in the order," Francois says, not even bothering to look at me.

"I'm not putting in the order. She's going to order something else for her meal. This is to tide her over."

"I cannot prepare if I do not have the order. It would ruin inventory when I have to reorder. I know you like to run this place like your personal kitchen, but it cannot be done."

I blow out a breath because I've been hearing the same thing from Francois over and over since I left the dishes in the sink three months ago and he knew I cooked in here late at night.

"Do you have any idea that you're not the boss?" I ask.

"I am the boss of the kitchen." He thumbs his chest.

"Stop using the fake French accent." He straightens his back, but I shake my head and go out onto the floor once more, snagging a basket of muffins and one of the carafes of coffee on my way. I set them both on my sisters' table. "Here."

"I can't drink coffee," Nikki says.

Thankfully, Rachel approaches them right after me and takes their order.

I see that Noah is now on a phone call, so I take a breather in the lobby.

Chevelle joins me a minute later and rubs my arm. "What am I missing? Are you okay?"

"Yeah, just overwhelmed. I mean, I've only met that guy once before."

"And?" Chevelle's face lights up as though she already knows what I'm going to tell her.

"It was literally one hour with him one night. Nothing big. We didn't exchange numbers or anything. I think he's kind of like a drifter or something."

"So?"

"So what's the point if nothing can happen long term?"

She scrunches up her face. "Mandi, who cares about the Noah thing? Nikki will get over it."

I shake my head. "No, it's because he travels so much for work."

She sets her hands on her hips. "When is the last time you did something for yourself? You can have a fling. No one has to know, and if they do, who cares? You're an adult."

Chevelle and I are complete opposites.

"Because I don't see the point in a fling that has no hope of ever becoming more."

"The point? How about hot, amazing sex. Three orgasms in a night. Imagine him coming back a few months apart. By the time you see him, you'd be climbing him like the tree he is. That man knows how to get a woman off, you can tell when you look at him."

We both lean over the partition and look at him. He's glancing around the restaurant and I hurriedly duck.

"I just don't know. I've never done anything like that." My voice sounds whiny and unsure.

"Live a little. Especially before you go and marry the perfect guy and have his perfect kids and live in that house with the white picket fence. It'll all be there waiting for you when you're ready. Go have fun." She nudges me with her arm.

I frown. "Maybe you're right."

"I am."

"Go, I've got you covered here," Trina says. "I need the extra hours anyway."

"Are you sure?"

She nods.

I inhale deeply. "Wish me luck."

"With those pants and that ass, you don't need luck." Chevelle smacks my ass and my cheeks heat before I even get out there.

Then the door of the restaurant dings and a tall brunette with mile-long legs says excuse me and slides past me.

"Noah," she says, waving, and I'm certain she's not talking about my soon-to-be nephew. She kisses him on the cheek and sits down, pulling the pancake plate in front of her.

All my sisters gawk and stare before slowly turning to look at me.

I shuffle back to my spot at the front desk. "Trina, you're done for the day."

"But—"

I shake my head. "Really, go get some rest. I'll see you this evening."

I need to stop thinking with my heart and go with my gut.

Noah

Eight months later...

I might be imagining things, but after my first encounter with Mandi, every time I've stayed at the inn, it seems like she's dodging me. And I think I might know why.

She wasn't there to check me in late last night. Trina, the middle-aged brunette, was polite enough at first, but when I asked where Mandi might be, she said it wasn't her job to keep track of her.

I sneaked out earlier this morning to take some pictures. I love my profession, but lately, I've felt plagued by the lack of freedom to shoot what I think is photoworthy. *National Geographic,* and other magazines like it, pay me for a specific job, and often what I see as beauty—like the snow hanging off the mountain—isn't as lucrative as two animals fighting, or an animal who's going extinct trotting along with her babies.

Squatting, I snap a picture of the slow, easy tide rolling into the bay.

"Is there something in the water?" A woman's voice distracts me.

When I turn around, I'm surprised to find a woman

dressed in scrubs sitting on the bench and drinking a coffee. I hadn't noticed her.

"No, just the water," I answer, getting up and leaning on a rock closer to her.

"Oh, so you're a photographer?"

I hold up my camera with a lens that definitely doesn't scream hobby.

She laughs. "Okay, you're a photographer. Do you take family photos?"

"N—" Before I answer, I stop myself. I *am* a little bored with what I've been doing lately, and the luxury of being a freelance photographer is that I can take time off whenever I want. "Not since school, but I—"

"My boyfriend and I have twins, Axel and Laurie." She sips her coffee. "I've wanted pictures of all of us for a while, but around here, it's hard to find someone who will do them. Especially if I want them outside and not in some stuffy studio."

"Okay."

"So, you'll do it?" She grins.

Now that she's offering me the job, I second-guess myself. "I'm probably rusty."

"Come on, please? My boyfriend is going to be a bear, I promise you, but you don't look like you'll be intimidated by him. And it would make me so happy. You don't want to disappoint a new mother, do you? I don't get any sleep, constantly feeding them. Oh!" She raises her hand as if we're in class. "I'm a nurse. If you're ever on the run and need stitches or something, I'm your girl."

I can't help but chuckle. "I'm not in the mob."

"You never know when you may find yourself in a tricky situation."

"I suppose."

"So will you do it? Are you a local? You don't look familiar, but I'm originally from Anchorage and, more recently, Lake Starlight. I've only been here a little less than a year."

I shake my head. "No. I'm just passing through."

That sounds suspicious. I could've said I'm from Greywall, but I never go there because it's exhausting to be in the middle of a family feud all the time.

"And how long are you here?" she asks.

"I leave the day after tomorrow."

"Perfect! My boyfriend has tomorrow off and that gives me time to get my hair done." She touches her dark hair. "How about we meet down here on the beach?" She quickly hops to her feet. "Oh, I have to go get outfits for all of us." When she pulls her phone out of her back pocket, we exchange numbers. "Does three work?"

"Sure."

"I'm so excited! Again, I apologize ahead of time for my boyfriend. He's the sheriff and kind of gruff." She leans forward. "I'll promise him something sexual to behave himself. Don't worry." She pats my arm, then she's walking up the ramp.

Following her, I spot Mandi peering down from the outside dining area of the inn. My stomach does some weird thing where it feels light and fuzzy. I lift my arm in a wave and she softly smiles, raising her hand. I put my camera away and walk up the steep hill to the inn.

"Hey," I say to Mandi when I'm close enough.

She crosses her arms and leans over the railing. "Hey."

"I've missed you the last couple times I've stayed at the inn."

"Sorry, had some family things come up."

I want to believe her, but I'm not sure I do. The last time we spoke was when Stacey met me here. The women at the table next to us kept giving us both an evil glare as though I'd offended them.

"I wanted to talk to you about something. Hang tight up there." I walk steadily to the door, checking my watch to make sure I have enough time before I have to go see my grandma.

Once I'm in the restaurant, I spot Mandi talking to a couple. I take the time to admire her without her knowing. During the long winter months, Mandi's face kept popping up in my head, especially late at night. She was like my sunshine, bringing light to the perpetual darkness. Her smile is contagious. She has one of those smiles that makes you want to make her laugh—sort of half smirk, half smile. To see her pink lips part and her long red hair fall back over her shoulders and know that you're responsible for making someone so beautiful laugh feels about as good as it gets.

But although my attraction to Mandi was instant and I feel as if I know her, it's absurd because we've only shared one night together. There's a lot working against us. My job being number one and her job being number two. I can't imagine living in the town next to Greywall. It's way too close to my parents, and you can't just up and move an inn that you own.

She says her goodbyes and walks toward me. Her head is always held high, her back straight. I find her confidence appealing. "Sorry, they come every year and I missed checking them in. Wanted to check up on them."

I shake my head. "No problem. You have to work." I stuff my hands in my pockets. "I just wanted to explain about Stacey."

"Stacey?" She raises her eyebrows.

"The woman who met me here in the restaurant that day. She's just a friend."

She's quick to wave me off. "That's none of my business, Noah."

"Still, I'd asked you to sit with me. She'd told me she was running late, and I was hoping to catch a few moments with you before she arrived."

A small blush creeps up her neck, and it only spurs me to keep divulging the truth.

"Then she came and I'm not sure... but were the three women sitting next to me... were they your sisters or something? I couldn't figure out why they kept giving me looks."

Her shoulders fall. "Yes, and ignore them. They believe in fairy tales. Expected your white horse to be tied up outside."

Does that mean Mandi's been talking about me as much as I've been thinking about her? I can't help the thrill that runs through me with that thought.

She leans in closer, looking around. "But I'm not that kind of woman."

I lean in even closer. "What kind of woman?"

"I'm not, like, a... a one-night stand woman. You float into town, we sleep together every time, but nothing real ever happens between us."

I rock back on my heels. "Well, my white horse might not be tied up outside, but I'm not really looking for a fling either. The problem is, there's no way I can entertain anything more right now. Just so we're on the same page." The disappointment I feel is crushing.

She smiles. "Great. So... friends?"

I've never hated a word more. "Friends." I thumb toward the door. "I have to go, but maybe tonight these friends could go on a walk?"

"Um... sure."

"I'll check in with you when I get back."

"Mandi!" the woman from the table from before calls to her.

"See you then." She waves and turns her back to me.

So that settles that. We're friends. I'm sure Mandi will be a great friend, as long as I can stop envisioning her naked.

I walk into Northern Lights Retirement Center, not surprised to find my grandma sitting on one of the couches in the living area, surrounded by a roomful of men. I love her zest for life and the fact that she's open about her needs as a woman, but sometimes I don't want to shake a man's hand at the retirement community because all I can think about is it being on my grandma.

"Noah," she says, and I bend down to give her a hug.

"Hey, Grandma." I hand her the bag of donuts she requested.

"Oh, thanks. Dori actually brought them for me yesterday. But I didn't want you to feel useless, so..." She hands them to the guy next to her whose head has fallen forward in sleep. "*Earl!* Wake up. Here are the donuts." She drops the bag in his lap and stands, but not before I notice her swipe a coaster from the table and slide it into her pocket.

She sees me notice and I shake my head at her. A few years ago when I noticed she started stealing stuff, I asked her about it and her exact words were, "I'm at the tail end of this schtick and I don't get much excitement in my life anymore. I like the rush of not knowing whether I'll get caught. Let an old gal live a little, will ya?"

My grandma gives me a look like she's daring me to challenge her for taking the coaster, but I just roll my eyes.

"Let's go to my room," she says. "We were up late last night so…"

"Nice. Playing cards?"

She glances back and pushes up her black-rimmed glasses. "Sure, sweetie. We were playing cards."

I inwardly shudder. Why do I even ask?

"Have you seen your parents?" She broaches the subject I don't care to discuss with her—ever.

"No. They don't know I'm in town this time."

She shakes her head. "Just passing through? Heading to the airport again?"

"Yeah." The lie tastes bitter on my tongue, but if Grandma knew how much time I spent here, she'd want more of it as well. This way no one in my family knows exactly how much time I'm spending with either.

"You need to settle down." She opens her apartment door and it smells like her perfume.

"Says the woman who can be found in a different man's bed every month." I raise an eyebrow.

She shakes her head. "I loved your grandfather, but I don't want to be married again. I've told you before, my sexual needs didn't change when your grandfather was buried. We had our time together, but it's done. My life has to continue until I join him."

"Yeah, I know, Grandma. My career doesn't allow me time to have a relationship anyway."

"I'm sure you could find some beautiful woman to follow you around to all those exotic places. You're young. That's what your youth is for." She sits in her glider chair where her feet don't touch the floor. "Want to watch *Price is Right*?"

"If you do." I check my watch. "I have to go soon."

"Always on the go. If I fix you up next time you come to town, will you go out with her?"

I shake my head. "No. I told you. I'm not going to entertain a relationship with anyone until I pull back on my career. I don't want the guilt when I go on excursions, and I don't want to ruin someone else's life because of it."

She shoos me with her hand. "You're way too practical. Just like your father."

"I'm nothing like him."

She must hear my tone because she backs down immediately. "No, you're not. I'm sorry. I shouldn't have said that."

"Maybe you should just reach out to him. You are his mother," I say for the millionth time since we're on the subject anyway.

"We've been over this. I'm his mother, he needs to come to me."

Always the same. I should be used to it by now, but it still feels like someone is twisting a dagger in my back.

I sit and watch fifteen minutes of *The Price is Right* before telling her I need to leave. After kissing her cheek, I walk down the hallway where Earl is now fully awake.

"Bye, son," he says.

I could be the protective grandson. But what am I going to do, tell him to watch her hip when they're between the sheets? I shake my head. "See ya, Earl."

On my way out, LeeAnn stops me at the front desk. "Noah, hey, we've been going over the paperwork and we need some forms filled out."

My grandma handles everything herself when it comes to the retirement community—mostly because when she entered, I was too young to be responsible for her. So my confusion must be obvious.

"We just need an updated emergency contact. Midge said she'd like you to be her point of contact."

I take the pen and see that there are two spots for emergency contacts. I fill out the first section, but they'll never reach me if I'm in the wilderness and cell service is horrible. LeeAnn leaves to go take a call, and while she's spouting off the amenities, I write down my dad's information for the second person. Flipping over the page, I put the pen on top and wave goodbye to LeeAnn.

The chances are slim that my dad would get a call, but maybe he needs to take a little responsibility for his mother after all these years he's stuck me in the middle.

Chapter Five

Mandi

The next day...

I walk out of the inn and spot my stepbrother, Fisher, and his girlfriend, Allie, with their twins.

"Hey, you two," I say, peeking into the stroller. "Laurie doesn't miss a thing, does she?" I poke her little belly.

"We're getting family photos done," Allie tells me.

I nod, because Fisher was already at my mom's and Hank's house while Allie was getting her hair done. News travels fast in our family. But I won't give away what I already know, and that's that Fisher picked up his mom's ring. After their mom passed away, each of the Greenes on Hank's side were given the opportunity to pick a piece of jewelry from their mom's collection to give to the woman they marry. As for Chevelle, I'm not sure how it worked for her.

"Perfect time of the day." I look over the bay where the sun is peeking behind the clouds but still visible.

"Is that the photographer?" Fisher points ahead of us. He stops walking and stares at Allie. "Tell me it isn't him."

I follow his line of sight and blink. "You're having Noah take your pictures?"

"You know him? He was taking some pictures of the bay

and the mountains yesterday when I came down here for some peace and quiet during my lunch shift."

"Did he hit on you?" Fisher asks. "I know you like facial hair."

Allie puts her arm around Fisher and pats his chest. "Relax, big guy." Then she looks at me. "We started to talk, and he showed me some of the pictures on his camera and I asked if he did family photos."

"And he said yes?" The question shouldn't sound so accusatory, but I had no idea he took family photos. A small bud of jealousy seems to be planted inside me.

Fisher's face twists. "I don't like this. He was hitting on you. I think he needs to know you belong to the sheriff."

"You guys, it's just family photos. I think he might work for *National*—"

"*Geographic*," I finish, not making eye contact with Allie.

"Yes!" Allie points as if we're playing a trivia game.

"Let's just get this over with. If he flirts or side-eyes you even once, it's on, Allie," Fisher grumbles and pushes the stroller down the pathway.

"I'll join you guys," I say without thinking how weird it might seem. "In case you need help getting the twins to cooperate."

"Thanks," Allie says, but I'm not looking at her. My eyes are on Noah squatting, taking pictures of the bay.

"I can't believe this. I thought it'd be a woman," Fisher grumbles. "Or some nerdy guy with glasses."

"Okay, Fisher, tone it down."

Noah spots us and his steady gaze stays on me. He's probably wondering why I'm here.

"Hi, Noah." Allie steps forward to shake his hand, and Fisher comes right up next to her. "This is Fisher."

"Her boyfriend. Father of her children." He puts out his big, meaty hand and Allie gives Noah an apologetic look.

They shake hands as Noah says, "Hey, nice to meet you. You'll have to bear with me, I've never photographed children before."

Fisher looks at Allie, but she ignores the heat of his stare on the side of her face.

"Hey, Mandi." Noah turns to me with a smile. He waves his finger between the three of us. "How do you guys know each other?"

"Fisher is my stepbrother." I nod in his direction.

"Small towns. Gotta love them, right? I come from one myself," Noah says.

Consider my interest piqued.

"Oh, really? Where?" Allie asks.

"I need to talk to you before we start," Fisher interrupts.

Fisher and Noah walk a few feet away, and Allie and I make conversation while we wait for them to rejoin us.

"Sometimes he's so caveman." Allie crosses her arms and shakes her head while the two men talk, then she busies herself with making sure Laurie's doing well while I try to slowly wake Axel so he's not a nightmare for the pictures.

"It seems weird that Noah agreed to do this," I say. The way he's talked about his landscapes and shooting in the wilderness, I never would've thought he'd take on a job like this.

A guilty look crosses Allie's face. "I did twist his arm a little. You know how hard it is to find photographers who shoot families in this area? Especially when the weather is nice."

I sit on the bench at the side of the path. "A lot of

photographers come through the inn throughout the year. You could've asked me."

She shrugs. "Hopefully this all works out."

Both men return and Allie's shoulders relax when it's clear that neither of them looks upset. Well, Fisher has a permanent resting-asshole face unless you're his family or friend, so I can't base my opinion on him, but Noah seems good.

"We're going to do you and Fisher first to make sure we get some good photos before we involve the babies." Noah fiddles with his camera.

Allie is quick to shoot down Noah. "Oh, I just wanted family, not us as a couple."

"We should have some of just the two of us," Fisher says, and Allie draws back. I'm surprised too. "Stop looking at me like that. Let's go."

Fisher places his hand in Allie's. The love between them is so transparent that a bud of hope grows a little more inside me. I can't deny that I want a man to look at me like that one day.

"Okay," Noah says, positioning Allie with her back to Fisher. "Perfect, Allie. And now Fisher."

Allie looks confused that Fisher isn't touching her. "Shouldn't—" Allie starts to move to glance over her shoulder, but Noah moves between her and Fisher.

"I'm trying to gauge the lighting and stuff, so just stay the way you are. I'll snap a few and then we'll get to posing you guys." Noah walks back to the babies and me.

Allie glances in my direction, her teeth on her bottom lip as though she's worried something is amiss. I'm trying to keep a straight face while I watch Fisher behind her. She deserves this surprise.

"Just like that, you two," Noah says, and Allie flashes a

quick smile. "Okay, go ahead and turn around, Allie, while I make sure everything looks good."

Allie turns toward Fisher, and her gaze falls to find him on bended knee with an open ring box on his palm.

"Fish," she whispers.

"I love you, Allie. I'm not sure how you did it, but you found me and loved me and brought me back to the land of the living. You're the best mom the twins could ask for and I want to make a million more babies with you. But most importantly, I want to spend every minute for the rest of my life loving you. Will you please be my wife?"

A tear trickles down her cheek. "I thought you didn't do marriage?"

"Keep giving me shit and I'll put the ring in my pocket." He holds it up higher. "Want me to count to three?" He raises his eyebrows.

"I swear I'm a saint for marrying you," she says and falls to her knees, holding out her left hand. "I guess I'm a glutton for punishment."

He takes out the ring and places it on the tip of her left ring finger. "I thought you were a smart girl."

"Me too."

"Well, this seals it. It's now or never?" He slides the ring onto her finger slowly as if she might say no.

"Just put it on."

He chuckles softly and slides it all the way down. "It looks beautiful on you."

Allie stares at the nontypical engagement ring that suits her so well. "Fish?"

"No take-backs."

"I love you, and I can't wait to spend the rest of my life with you." She smacks her lips on his and he loses balance and they both fall to the ground.

"I promise I'll give you a great life." He tucks her hair behind her ear.

"You've given me everything I could ever want."

He looks at her quizzically.

"You gave me your heart and two healthy babies. That's enough for me," she says.

He places his hands on her cheeks and kisses her until I clear my throat.

"Marla and my dad are babysitting tonight, so I plan to show you exactly what your future will be—orgasm style."

"I can't wait."

"Babies! You guys already have two," I holler, not sure why they think people can't hear them. "And one is fussy."

Fisher gets up on his feet and holds his hand out for Allie.

"You got all that?" Fisher asks Noah.

"Yeah." Noah smiles. "Congratulations."

"Let me see!" I practically run over to Allie. "Wait until everyone finds out I got to see Fisher propose. They're going to be so jealous." I take Allie's hand so I can see the ring. "This was your mom's?" I ask Fisher while admiring the ring. I've never seen one like it before.

"Yeah."

"What?" Allie asks quietly, her emotions obviously choking her.

Fisher gets Laurie out of the carrier. She's started squawking her displeasure. "We all picked an item of jewelry from my mom's collection to pass on to our significant other someday. I picked that ring a long time ago." He walks over to Allie with Laurie in his arms.

"But you said..."

"Weird, right? When I went over to get it from Dad

today... I didn't even remember exactly what it looked like, but it's perfect for you. Like it was destiny or something."

I want to ask if someone has taken over Fisher's body. Is this what love does to someone? Makes them believe in destiny and fate and rescuing hearts?

Allie nods and more tears spill from her eyes. "It is."

"I guess my younger self knew something I didn't." He kisses her temple. "Let's get these family photos over with so we can get a room."

"Deal." She kisses him and grabs Axel.

Noah apologizes the entire time he's taking their pictures, but watching him work—the way his finger clicks, the perfection as he maneuvers the lens, walking around them, squatting, standing on a bench—you just know he's seeing things behind that lens that others wouldn't, which makes him a genius.

Once they're finished, I say goodbye to everyone and walk back up to the inn. Noah jogs to catch up to me.

"Love, huh?"

I side-glance him. "I never thought I'd see Fisher fall so far, so fast, but it's nice."

He nods, swinging his bag up his shoulder. "I can see how if someone was a wedding photographer, they'd really believe in love."

"Do you not?"

He shrugs. "There's no reason for me not to."

"What do you mean?"

"Well, my parents are still married. My grandparents were married until my grandpa passed. There's no deep dark reason to why I wouldn't. But would I ever find someone who would make me want to give up my career?" He shrugs again. "Seems impossible."

"Isn't true love supposed to help you reach your dreams?" That's what I would want.

"How could she do that when I'm barely around? And what kind of true love am I if I ask her to drop her own life to follow me?"

I nod, understanding exactly what he's saying. If someone asked me to give up my inn because their life was somewhere else, I'm not sure love would be enough for me to do it either.

After all, unlike Noah, I did witness a love disintegrate and crumble under lies and deceit. I watched my mother give up all her dreams for love and try to reinvent herself years later after the ugly side of love had reared its head.

Noah

Four months later...

Afer returning from Bali, I arrive at the SunBay Inn only to find out that Mandi's gone on vacation. I blame my disappointment on the fact that it was mostly couples in Bali. I had been contracted to take pictures of a new resort for their brochures and online presence. Staying in one of the huts over the ocean was awesome, something I'm not used to since most of my work is in the middle of nowhere. Seeing all the couples talking over candlelight dinners and strolling the beach made me yearn for one of my conversations with Mandi.

Although we haven't had a lot of deep ones, she's easy to talk to, and she never pushes past my boundaries for information I'm not ready to share. Hell, she still doesn't know I'm from Greywall.

I'm in my room, wondering if I should pack my bag and head to New York City and spend the week with friends, when my phone rings. I groan, seeing my grandma's name on the screen. Sliding my thumb over, I put it on speaker.

"Hi, Grandma."

"Oh good, I got you. Where are you? Home?"

"Sort of, yes." I don't directly answer because neither my

grandma nor my parents know I rent out my place in Grey-wall full time. I used to stay there when I was in town but decided it was easier to rent it out all the time and just stay at the inn whenever I'm in town.

"Oh good. Be a dear and come get me and my friends and drive us to the airport."

I sigh. "What would you do if I wasn't around?"

She laughs. "I keep your itinerary in my head. Knew you'd be home and I just forgot to let you know we were counting on you. I'm old, give me a break. Now come on. My friends are paying for me to go, and I want to do something nice for them. Get over here before one of their grandsons do, okay? Make me look good."

There's no way she'd let me say no, and I'm really not doing much, so whatever.

"Sure. I'll be there in twenty."

"Make it fifteen and I'll give you a nice tip."

"I'm your grandson. I'm not going to charge you," I say, swiping my keys off the table.

"I didn't say the tip would be money. See you soon."

Click.

"Okay then," I murmur to myself.

I drive over to Northern Lights Retirement Center, and sure enough, the three grandmas are sitting outside with their luggage, staring me down as if I'm their late Uber driver.

"Ladies," I say and help each of them climb into the truck. I pick up their luggage and put it in the back.

When I get back into the truck, the three women are talking about how they wonder if the retirement center will survive without them.

"To the airport, ladies?"

"Yes, thank you, Noah. This means a lot to us," Ethel says from the back seat.

"You're welcome."

We ride the entire way with them gossiping about various family members. Dori is upset about something one of her grandsons did, and Ethel's saying she'd take him over the knee for it. Then they're talking about some Hank and Marla people, and I figure out that Hank must be Ethel's son because she mentions how she feels guilty for being healthy when her son is sick.

I try to refrain from joining in, and thankfully Grandma doesn't drag me into the mix.

Then I hear Ethel say, "I'm going to message Mandi. She'll meet us at departures and get us where we need to go."

My eyes instinctually shift to the rearview mirror. Ethel doesn't have red hair, and I'm sure Mandi from SunBay Inn isn't the only Mandi in the area.

"Yeah, you know her time is coming," Dori chimes in, and I swear her eyes meet mine in the mirror.

I quickly return my focus to the road. After all, I don't want to be the guy who gets three elderly women into a car accident. I'd never hear the end of it from any of these three.

"She's going to be a stubborn one." Ethel is concentrating on her phone. "Likes things a certain way."

"But she'll make a great mother and wife someday with how organized and responsible she is." Dori leans over and whispers something into Ethel's ear.

Meanwhile, my grandma is humming to Whitesnake because she turned my satellite radio station to the eighties channel like she always does.

"Oh believe me, I bet that girl is one of those," Ethel says.

I lean farther back in my seat to try to hear them.

"Really?" Dori asks, her gray eyebrows raised.

"There's a little bit of that girl in all of us," Ethel says.

Both women laugh, then they look in the rearview mirror.

Thankfully, Grandma belts out, "Sweet lip honey be the death of me."

"Midge!" Ethel scolds.

Dori laughs and elbows Ethel. "A little bit of that girl in all of us. Some of us a little more than others."

"Whoops, sorry. Your grandfather loved this song." She looks at me dreamily with her cheek on the seat cushion.

Although I'm thoroughly creeped out by this, I do see how much Grandma misses him.

Finally, I get off the highway, following the signs to the departure area. I stop along the curb and flag down a skycap to check them in, figuring that will help whoever from Ethel's family is coming to get them through security, but of course my grandma is the one who demands the skycap not take her bag.

"I told you, I got it." Grandma tears a bag away from one of the skycaps.

"Midge, he's just trying to help," Ethel says.

"This has all my medicine in it."

The skycap puts up both hands, and I figure this is my time to step in.

"Relax, Noah, I'm fine." Grandma pushes past me, pushing my shoulder and causing me to spin around.

My eyes lock with the woman standing behind us.

Mandi.

Guess maybe there aren't that many Mandis in the immediate area.

She's with a blonde who stops walking and looks between us. "Do you know him?"

"Mandi." I can't stop my smile, and seeing her own grin at our impromptu meeting only sparks my interest more. "What are you doing here?" Which is a stupid question because I've already figured it out.

She points at the grandmas. "I'm getting them."

The blonde rushes over to help clear up whatever the problem is, informing the skycap what flight they're on. She pretty much handles it like a pro, and neither Mandi nor I have to intervene except to tell Ethel she can't take her knitting needles in her carry-on.

"I'm not going to stab someone," she says.

I clear my throat behind Mandi. Her neck cranes from looking up at me. All I want to do is run my hand to the back of her neck to tilt her head up so I can kiss the living shit out of her.

"Is this some volunteer thing?" I ask.

"Like I'd voluntarily agree to take three elderly women to Hawaii to be badgered about being—" She cuts off her sentence. I get the same crap from my grandma all the damn time.

"Noah, thanks for the ride." Dori pats my cheek. "Next time though, fifteen minutes before planned. You never know with traffic."

I halfheartedly smile at her, not having the heart to rat my grandma out for forgetting to tell me to pick them up. "Got it, Bluehaze."

Dori laughs and shakes her head. "The nicknames and this guy." She thumbs in my direction.

"Hi, I'm Clara." The blonde extends her hand, and my eyes meet hers as we shake hands.

"You're a volunteer too?" I ask, then turn my attention

back to Mandi.

"Noah thinks we're chaperoning Ethel and her friends willingly," Mandi says with a smile.

Clara giggles. "Sure, I've got a suitcase full of Bengay and overnight diapers."

"If not just being nice, what gives?" I shouldn't pry, but I have to know exactly how Mandi is related.

"It's a Greene family vacation and my grandma"—she points in Ethel's direction—"invited her two friends to come along. She said she can't keep up with all our energy, so she needs friends to play cards with."

"Which really means to gossip and get into trouble with," Clara adds.

"You two both single?" I point my finger between them.

Mandi groans. "Unfortunately, yes."

I touch her arm. "I'm sorry. Every available man will know within five minutes of you arriving at the hotel." Why does the thought of that make me grind my teeth?

"Right?" Mandi cringes. "I could stow you away. We could always pretend."

We all laugh.

"This was one ride you should have declined, right?" Clara says.

"What do you mean?" I ask.

"You're their Uber driver, no?"

"No." I shake my head, realizing I haven't told them how I fit into all this. "I'm Midge's grandson."

"Oh," Clara says.

As if Grandma heard us, she comes over. "Bend down so I can kiss your cheek."

I do as I'm asked, and she leaves her signature berry-pink lipstick on my cheek above where my beard line stops.

"Be a good boy while I'm gone. No excursions?"

I glance at Mandi and back down at Grandma. "Not until October."

"Good. I like you being home."

"Where's home?" Mandi is quick to ask.

I want to rush my grandma away, hell, pay a skycap a hundred to take her away right now, but of course she beats me to answering.

"Greywall of course," Grandma says in a tone that implies Mandi's stupid.

The two women look at one another and raise their eyebrows.

"We gotta go," Ethel says from the entrance of the airport, forcing everyone else trying to enter to walk around her. "Thanks, Noah. See you on the flip side."

"Flip side?" Mandi mouths.

I laugh, knowing the next time I see Mandi I'll have a million questions to answer. "Have fun, you two. Too bad there's not an extra ticket."

"Yeah, too bad," Mandi murmurs.

"Nice meeting you, Noah. Wish us luck," Clara says.

After a wave, I stand there until they disappear through the glass sliding doors.

"Sir! Sir!" The airport attendant rushes over. "You can't park here."

"I'm going. I'm going."

I strip my eyes from Mandi and Clara, almost wishing I was going on vacation with them. Not because of the grandmas but because I wouldn't mind seeing Mandi in a bathing suit. I bet all her curves would look hot as fuck. Then my mind floods with images of what her style might be. Starting the engine of my truck, I attempt to shake off the visions in my head of a scantily clad Mandi.

It's times like this I wonder if traveling all over the world is really worth it. I mean, I've always thought it was amazing to see different things, experience a bunch of cultures, and meet all kinds of people. But lately, those things don't fill the need inside me to be surrounded by people who truly know and care for me. But even that's hard to find in Alaska when your parents and your grandma can't be in the same room together. Speaking of, while Grandma is gone, I might as well go to dinner with my parents.

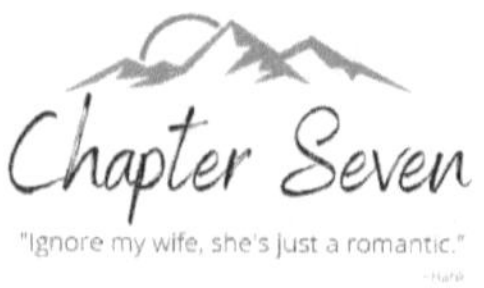

Noah

I decide to kill some time in Greywall since I'm not booked for a job for a few months. With Grandma on her trip to Hawaii with Ethel's family, I don't feel as much guilt as normal at the idea of seeing my parents. I shouldn't feel guilty, I know, but they've all put me in the middle of this family feud. I feel guilty when I'm with my grandma and I feel guilty when I'm with my parents. There's no winning.

Walking into my childhood home, the smell of oil paints is a welcoming scent and reminds me of better times, when our family dynamic wasn't as strained as a piano wire. My dad always painted, even when the company was still in the family. Back then it was just a hobby.

"Mom? Dad?" I call.

No one answers because more than likely, they're in two different rooms.

I head to my mom's workspace first, knocking lightly before opening the door. Her music of choice—which is soft jazz—is playing, so I assume she's lost in creating her art. Rounding the corner, I anticipate finding her on her stool, a streak of paint in her dark, curly hair.

"Mom?"

"Noah?" Her voice sounds strained.

"Yeah." I continue around the corner into her little makeshift art studio. "Oh god!"

My mom is on a divan, legs spread open and her hand... oh Jesus. I circle around and head in the other direction.

"Give us a second," she calls, but I'm already out the door.

I walk right to the kitchen and open the fridge, looking for any drop of alcohol I can find, but of course there's nothing. After watching his dad drink too much growing up, he vowed never to have alcohol in the house. So I settle for a Coke and sit at the kitchen table, hoping like hell that image will one day leave my mind.

"He's old enough to understand his parents have sex, Ursula." My dad's voice is the first I hear. "Not to mention it's art. I was drawing your beautiful figure."

"Oh come on, Rex, you know as well as I do, no boy wants to see his mother with her legs spread open."

I wince, staring at my hands clasping the Coke can in front of me. Their footsteps approach and they each sit in a chair opposite me.

My mom reaches out and I pray it's not the hand she was... oh hell, I can't even think about it. "I'm sorry, Noah. We weren't expecting you."

"It was a surprise visit."

"Well, a call would be nice," my dad says.

I look at him. "Like I said, I was surprising you."

My dad rolls his eyes and I down a hefty gulp of my drink.

"What brings you by?" my mom asks, always the bridge between my dad and me.

I shrug. "I'm around for a little bit. Thought I'd see how you two are doing."

"And how was Bali?" My mom leans back in her seat, crossing her legs and pulling her robe over her bare limbs.

"Could you put some clothes on?" I cringe.

She sighs but stands. "I'll be right back." She places her hand on my shoulder and disappears down the hall of my parents' modest ranch-style home.

"Do you need money?" my dad asks once my mom is gone.

I haven't asked him for anything since I graduated college and needed to borrow money for a decent used camera.

I look hard at him. "No. Why would you ask that?"

"Because you don't usually like spending time with us. From what I've gathered over the years, you prefer to be with your grandma."

I blow out a breath and massage my temples for a second. Here we go again. "No, I'm just constantly stuck between the two of you."

He says nothing, knowing it's the truth. Ever since my grandpa died when I was seventeen, my close-knit family imploded, fracturing into two sides, with me in the middle. Grandma sold off the family company and moved into Northern Lights Retirement Center and my dad has resented her ever since.

"Forget I said anything. Want to go out to eat tonight? There's a new restaurant that opened, owned by the same guy who owns Terra and Mare in Lake Starlight. I'll call and see if I can get us in." He stands and picks up their landline phone. They're the only people I know with one these days.

My mom returns dressed in shorts and a blouse. "So, tell me about Bali. Don't you have the best life ever?"

"It was beautiful."

"That's all you have to say?"

I shrug. "The water was clear, the sand perfectly white. It's paradise."

"You need someone to share these things with?" She poses it as a question.

"No, we've been over this. As long as I'm photographing around the world, I'm not getting into a serious relationship." I gulp down the rest of my Coke.

She leans back in her chair, crossing her legs and tapping her fingers on the table while her dark eyes inspect me. "There are a lot of women who would love to travel the world with you."

I think about how awesome it would be to find someone who would travel with me, but that would mean asking her to put her own life on pause. I could never do that. "Maybe so, but there's not one I've found who interests me."

"You know I'm only getting older, right? I'd like grandchildren one day. I want to see you happy."

"Imagine how happy Grandma was when you had me."

She retracts her hand from the table, crossing her arms and narrowing her eyes at me. "Don't make me feel guilty over something I have no control over." She glances at my dad.

My dad is still talking on the phone with the restaurant, so I figure I have one last shot with my mom before he returns. "You have some control. She's only getting older, you know. And it's all over such a stupid thing."

"Millions of dollars and a family legacy isn't a stupid thing. We all know your grandfather wanted the business kept in the family. And that money could've done a lot for this family... for you."

"Aren't you guys happy now?"

A soft smile creases her lips, and she looks at my dad.

"We are. But we would've have been happy with that life too."

"It's all set," my dad says, joining us. "The three of us at the new restaurant in town. I've been hearing great things about it."

As always, the conversation dies, and I've gotten nowhere in pushing my parents to make amends with my grandma, the same as I did when I tried with my grandma.

AFTER DINNER WITH MY PARENTS, I go back to SunBay Inn and say hello to Trina behind the front desk before climbing the stairs to my room.

After minutes in my room, I'm restless, so I grab my camera and head out.

The difference between Greywall and Sunrise Bay is the nightlife. Maybe it's the Truth or Dare Brewery or the fact that the town hosts more activities, but when I step outside of the inn and walk up the hill toward downtown, I hear the sounds of life.

The cobblestone streets, which are restricted from cars, give the small town a more intimate feel than the neighboring ones. I sit in front of The Grind at a black iron table, and I snap some pictures of the busy businesses. The crowd waiting to get into Truth or Dare, the couples grabbing a late-night coffee and walking in and out of the small shops that line the street.

I catch a little guy with an ice cream cone that has more ice cream dripping down his arm than he's probably managed to get in his mouth. His mom is constantly trying to wipe his face until the dad takes the mom's hand and says something I assume is along the lines of "forget it, let's enjoy the night."

"It's a great town, right?" A dark-haired woman sits down next to me. There's something familiar about her, but I can't place it. "I grew up here and moved away, only to return years later and fall in love with it all over again."

"It really is a great place." I snap pictures of a woman staring at the sky and circling around until her date grabs her by the waist. She laughs, and they walk in the direction of the inn.

"This is my favorite time of the year here. When tourist season is at its peak and Mother Nature gifts us these perfect nights."

I smile at her.

"So where are you from?" she asks.

"All over."

"Are you a photographer?" She nods toward the camera in my hands.

"I am, so it takes me a lot of places." I continue to stare through my lens, waiting to line up my next shot.

"I bet you'll never find a place like Sunrise Bay. It's unique."

I chuckle under my breath. I think every person who lives in a small town either hates it or loves it, and the ones who love it always think it's the best town ever. "Why is that?"

"There's love everywhere. Most of my children have all fallen in love in this town, found their one and only. I reunited with my first love years later when I returned. Stay long enough and there'll be a ring on that finger of yours." She eyes my hand, and my grasp on the camera tightens.

A tall man approaches. "Ignore my wife, she's just a romantic."

"In fact"—the woman ignores the man—"I have a daughter who I think would be perfect for you. Are you interested in a blind date?"

The man holds out his hand. "Let's leave this man to his night, honey."

She accepts his hand and stands, and he instantly puts his arm around her waist and kisses the top of her head.

"She's sweet and beautiful and everything this town represents," the woman adds.

"Thank you, but I'm not looking for anyone right now."

She frowns for a moment. "A nonbeliever, huh?"

"Let's go." The man tries to direct her away.

"I'm not a nonbeliever. I just don't have the time. I travel way too much."

She looks at who I assume is her husband. "Excuses, that's what those are. When you find the one, all those obstacles just disappear. You figure it out. We blended two families. Had two sons at each other's throats, a nightmare of an ex-husband to deal with, and four daughters fighting over bathrooms and bedrooms. If you want to be together, you make it work."

He smiles at her. "I wouldn't change a thing."

"Me either."

They stare into each other's eyes for a moment, and it's endearing, the love they share. I get why she'd want that for her children and anyone (even strangers) she meets.

"You two are obviously in love. Thanks for sharing with me. Now if you don't mind—"

"Please go ahead," the man says with a nod toward the Truth or Dare Brewery. "Tell the bartender your drink is on his old man."

I shrug with a smile. "Okay."

"Have a good night," the woman says.

"Come on, you, let me take you home." The man leads her toward the other side of downtown and they disappear.

I've never been in Sunrise Bay for very long. Usually I'm passing through for a night or two, and even then, I'm so exhausted from traveling and being on excursions that I don't explore much. So I figure why not enjoy myself and see what's so unique about this small town that neighbors my own.

Mandi

Two months later...

When I stepped off the plane a couple months ago, I was relaxed, as if I had just been massaged from head to toe. That's not the case anymore. I came home to a stack of bills that need to be paid. I haven't fallen behind yet, but tourist season was down for me compared to prior years.

I push away all those pressures, walking into the auction Clara is having to raise funds for the library extension. Even with business being slow, I donated an item because that's what you do in a small town.

My stepbrother, Xavier, is already seated, his body tense and stiff. I take the seat next to him and he glances in my direction. We joke around about the grandmas in the front row before Clara bangs the gavel for everyone to quiet.

Clara auctions off what I think are all the items, and I'm about to get out of my seat when she continues. "For our next item, we've been donated something extremely unique and special. To explain each item in better detail than I could, let me bring up the talented man responsible."

"Shut up," I murmur.

"What?" Xavier asks.

"Everyone, this is Noah," Clara says.

"As in our nephew?" Xavier laughs, but I'm flabbergasted.

My eyes follow Noah's journey up the narrow path of plastic chairs. He's dressed in dark clothes with his hair pulled back again.

"Who's he?" Xavier asks.

"Midge's grandson."

"And we like Midge's grandson?"

I turn to hide my blush.

"Do we like Midge's grandson?"

"Shut up, Xavier. We don't. He's just... he just spends some time at the inn on occasion."

"Okay." Xavier says nothing else, but I know what he's thinking.

Noah goes up to the podium and I realize how petite Clara looks next to him. I wonder what the two of us look like to everyone when we're next to each other. Lord knows I'm a lot curvier than Clara.

Noah picks up a framed photo and places it on an easel. "This is a picture of a moose lying down with the mountains behind it."

He explains where he took the shot and how hard it was to capture. And that's not all he's got. For the next fifteen minutes, Clara auctions off framed art of a bald eagle with its wings spread, flying in the air; a bear and her cub fishing for salmon in a river; wolf packs; and sea lions. All while Noah explains where and how he got each shot.

"The man is talented," Xavier mumbles.

"Yeah, he is."

"I wonder if he's as talented in other areas." Xavier waggles his eyebrows, and I elbow him in the ribs.

The pictures go for what I'm sure is less than Noah is

used to getting, but what is still a huge amount of money for the people in this town.

Clara heads back up to the podium. "Okay, that's all for tonight. I can't thank—"

"Nope. I have my own donation." My grandma stands.

Xavier and I share a look because this can't be good. I don't know exactly what *this* is, but I know it's not good—for someone.

"Oh, Ethel, I didn't know. I'm sorry. What is it?" Clara says, always the polite one.

Grandma looks around the room until her gaze stays on Xavier.

"Shit," he says under his breath.

"My grandson, Xavier. A dinner with him. He's the quarterback of the Kingsmen down in San Francisco. Come on, ladies. Now's your chance."

I can't stop laughing as Xavier goes up to the front.

I watch with amusement as my grandma tries to sell off a major league quarterback, and a body sits down in the chair Xavier just left. I glance over and smile at Noah. He smiles back and I feel the familiar flutter in my stomach. This game we play feels as if it's become complicated. I should not be thinking this often about someone I consider just a friend.

He leans over. "Want to get something to eat after this?"

I nod. "Sure." I keep my voice even, but inside I'm squealing.

We wait until Xavier is auctioned off to the least likely person I would've imagined, then we step out of the building into the crisp autumn night.

"Where to?" Noah asks.

I shrug. With tourist season nearly finished, we don't have a ton of options, so we head to Truth or Dare Brewery.

"Who was the guy sitting next to you?" he asks once

we're seated at the table farthest from the bar, which is nice. I don't want anyone who works here to eavesdrop.

"Just my stepbrother."

"Xavier Greene is your stepbrother?" His eyes widen.

My head tilts. "If you knew him, why did you ask?"

I spot Jed cleaning the table next to us. I really wish none of them were here tonight because Noah is about to get a crash course on how big my family really is.

He shrugs. "I didn't know what he was to you. I mean, yeah you have the same last name, but there's gotta be a lot of Greenes in the world. Didn't mean you were related."

I raise both eyebrows.

"I was gonna tell you that he's got feelings for the blonde on stage."

"And how do you know that?"

"I think it was clear to everyone in that room. I just wouldn't want you to be played."

We're interrupted by a chair scraping across the floor as Jed turns it around and straddles it. "Hey there."

I shake my head. Noah glances at me before setting his focus back on Jed.

"Mandi?" Jed asks, his pen poised over his paper.

"I'll just have a Razzle Dazzle."

"And your guest?" He turns his attention to Noah.

Noah's eyes narrow, but he picks up the small drink menu. "The flight."

"Anything else?" Jed stares at me.

"Give us a minute to look at the menu." I give him a smile I hope conveys "get the hell out of here."

Jed taps his pen on his pad. "Sure thing."

Then he leaves and I can breathe again.

Until Noah asks, "Do we know the waiter?"

"That's Jed Greene, my brother."

"How many Greenes live in this town?"

I add them up in my head. "Well, I have three full siblings and five stepsiblings. Most are married now. Add on my mom and her husband—"

"Wait. Does your mom have dark hair and her husband is a taller guy with dark hair, a little gray in it? She the kind who might lecture a stranger about how romantic this town is?"

I laugh. "Sounds like her."

"I met her while you were on vacation."

"Yeah, they couldn't go because my stepdad is going through treatment for prostate cancer. I'm surprised she didn't try to fix you up with someone. She's starting to take after my stepgrandma, Ethel."

Noah shakes his head. "It's crazy how intermingled our lives are, but we didn't even know it."

Jed brings over our drinks and we each order quesadillas since I push Noah to order their specialty. Jed lingers, so I figure I might as well start the introductions.

"Jed, this is Noah. Noah, this is my brother, Jed."

The two men shake hands and it's weird. I've always thought of Noah as my secret. Not that I want to keep him a secret, but introducing him to my family feels like inviting him to play an even bigger role in my life, which is unsettling.

They exchange pleasantries before Jed has to go help some more customers.

"Jed and my stepbrother Cade own this place."

Noah nods. "So everyone in your family stayed in Sunrise Bay?" The disbelief in his tone doesn't surprise me, since I just found out he's from Greywall.

"Yeah. Except Xavier—he comes and goes. Two of my sisters even married people who relocated their lives here."

He sips one of the beers from his flight. "Interesting. So I assume you'll marry someone who wants to stay in town someday?"

I shrug. "Honestly?"

"Always."

"I'm not sure whether I'll even get married. I might be the complete opposite of my mom."

"Why would a woman like you not believe in love?"

"A woman like me?" I raise an eyebrow.

He chuckles. I love the sound of his deep laugh. "Gorgeous, and let's be honest, you'd make one hell of a wife."

I wish his compliment didn't make me blush, but my cheeks instantly heat. Redheads have a hard time hiding when they blush.

Not many men have called me gorgeous. Maybe because society's perception of larger women isn't always gorgeous or beautiful. In a small town like ours, I've watched all my sisters be flirted with and asked out when most of the guys I've known have put me in the friend zone. That's not why I don't believe in love though. That has everything to do with my parents' divorce.

Noah just makes me forget that I don't believe in love because when he looks at me the way he is right now, I want to say screw it and straddle him in the chair, kissing him until we have to tear ourselves apart for a deep breath.

"Why do you assume I'd make a good wife?"

He sips his beer and leans back in the chair. "I've never met someone so caring. I've seen the way you take care of your guests. It's like it comes naturally, like it's instinct for you."

"Well, I don't give everyone two chocolates at turndown."

We both laugh.

"I wondered if I was special."

He is, much as I hate to admit it. Once again, the thought of having just one night with him crosses my mind. Surely I'm someone who can put aside the worry that I'd grow close to him and get hurt in the end.

"Tell me more about you."

He blows out a breath. "Like?"

"Like why you stay at my inn when you're in town when you're from Greywall?"

He bites his lip and nods, staring at the busy tables. "I come to see my parents and my grandma on occasion. They're the only family I have. The problem is the two of them don't get along. At all. They don't even speak to each other anymore."

My forehead creases. "Really? Midge?"

He nods. "They haven't said a word to one another since I was seventeen."

"Why?" Realizing how nosy I'm being, I raise my hands. I hate when people ask me personal things when they barely know me. "Never mind. None of my business."

"No, it's okay." He waves off my backtracking. "My grandfather died when I was seventeen and my grandma was left everything in the will. Including the mining business that had been in our family for generations. She sold it off without consulting my dad. After that, my dad cut her off. I'm not sure how my mom really feels, but she took my dad's side, obviously. And I got stuck in the middle. So I stay at the SunBay Inn because it's a retreat where they'd never look for me. I do a dinner here or a lunch there with each of them. But always separately."

"That's gotta be hard." I place my hand on his forearm.

His large hand lands on mine and goose bumps race up my arm.

Just keep ignoring these feelings, Mandi. It's what you do best.

Of course, Jed picks that moment to deliver our food. His gaze lingers where we're touching. And Jed being Jed, he sits down. "I'm sorry, Noah, where did you say you're from?"

"Jed," I say with zero patience in my tone.

But my brother doesn't shift his gaze from Noah's.

I slide my hand out from under Noah's as he says, "I'm originally from Greywall, but I travel for work now. I do a lot of shoots for *National Geographic*."

"You're the photographer?" Jed asks as though he's heard rumors about him.

"Yeah."

"I heard you did Fisher and Allie's family photos?"

My mouth drops open. Here I thought Jed was going to go all big protective brother on him.

"My girlfriend is pregnant, and I have a seven-year-old. Do you do a lot of family photos?"

Noah appears a little uncomfortable. "Um, it's not really my specialty."

"Oh." Jed stands.

"But sure." Noah digs out his wallet and pulls out his card, passing it to my brother. "Give me a call to set up a time."

Jed accepts the card and smiles at me. "Great. Molly's had horrible morning sickness and I want to do something special for her. I figure pictures are forever."

"True enough," Noah says.

"I'll probably wait until she's almost full term, but I'll be in touch. 'Kay, now I'll leave you two to it." He winks at me, and I groan.

"At this rate, it seems like I'll be the family portrait guy if I stay in this town long enough." He takes another drink from his flight.

"Would that be a bad thing?" I ask more for myself than him and wish I could take it back.

Noah locks eyes with me. "I'm not sure. I used to think so."

Neither of us shifts our gaze, and I try to decipher his words. Am I the one making him unsure now, or is it that he's grown bored with wildlife photography? He did mention it being lonely once.

I strip my gaze from him. "We should eat before it gets cold."

"Yeah. Good thinking."

We enjoy our meal, and afterward, we walk back to the inn. I say good night to him and get in my car to drive back to my place, though that's not really what I want to do.

Noah

Three months later...

I can't deny that Mandi is tempting as hell. The closer we get, the more I keep having to remind myself that she's off-limits.

The fact that I stop in Sunrise Bay more than ever says I'm only asking for trouble.

Like tonight, I could've gone to the airport and caught a flight to New York, but here I am, outside the inn at my usual time, eleven at night. The problem is, I don't have a reservation this time. I was on my way to the airport when I turned around. What the hell was I thinking?

I turn off my truck and sit there staring at the one light on in the reception area. Her car is parked alongside the building, out of the way of guest parking.

"Fuck it," I say, grabbing my suitcase from the back seat.

At least it isn't raining.

The bell rings when I open the door and I smile because I can't wait to see her, but when I look, she's not behind the desk.

"Just a minute," she calls.

I approach the desk, still unable to stop smiling because I can't wait to see her reaction. I'm hoping she'll be as excited as I am. It's not like we're dating, but we're definitely flirting.

"So sorry." She comes out from the back office but doesn't look up right away. "Can I help you?" She lifts her head, and her stunning hazel eyes are red rimmed and her cheeks stained from tears.

"Mandi?" I drop my suitcase and round the reception area.

"Noah?" She swipes under her eyes. "What are you doing here? I didn't see a reservation for you." She ignores my closeness and types into the computer as though she missed it.

"I was going to head home to New York, but I wanted to see you."

She blinks a couple of times and looks at me. "See me?"

I nod. "What's wrong?"

She shakes her head. Anyone who really knows Mandi knows she sees her problems as hers and hers alone. She'll never burden someone else with them.

"Come on. Tell me." I open my arms, but she doesn't walk into them. Gotta admit, that stings a little.

"It's nothing. Here, let me check you in."

"Mandi, no, tell me what's going on," I plead. I go over to the front door, flip the closed sign, and lock it.

"Come on." I grab her hand before she can check me in and take her into the dining room. Pulling out a chair, I wait for her to sit before sliding it back in toward the table. "Talk to me."

Her head is down, and I see a tear fall into her lap. I sit in the chair next to hers and wait for her to talk.

"It's just the business. It was a hard winter."

"How hard?"

Her fingers twine together, and I notice her pink nail

polish is chipped, which usually isn't the case. I wonder if she's been picking at them all night. "It's nothing, Noah. Nothing you need to be concerned about."

"I'm your friend, aren't I?"

"A friend who doesn't need to know his friend's business is failing."

My chest tightens. "Tourist season is coming. We can brainstorm some ideas. Get you completely booked. We can fix this."

She shakes her head. "Thank you, but this is my problem. I'll handle it." She rises out of the chair. "Help yourself to the kitchen if you're hungry."

"Accept my help," I call, but she returns to the reception area and goes through the office door, shutting it and sealing off her decision.

I sit at the table for a moment until my cell phone vibrates in my pocket.

It's my dad's number, so I pick it up. "Dad?"

"Where the hell have you been? Your grandmother had a heart attack. We're in Lake Starlight, at the hospital."

All the air leaves my lungs. "I'll be right there."

I hang up and knock on the office door. Mandi opens it, and I see the pile of tissues in her trash can.

"I have to go, but if you need me, call me, okay? I'll be back in a little while." I take her limp hand and squeeze.

"You're very sweet. I'll be fine. I always am."

I wish I could stay, but I squeeze her hand one more time before letting it go. Then I grab my suitcase and head out to my truck to rush to the hospital.

By the time I reach the hospital, my dad is pacing the entrance, which tells me that either my grandma died or he's planning on hightailing it outta here as soon as I arrive.

"Please explain to me why I'm getting these phone calls?"

I stuff my hands in my pockets. "They needed two emergency numbers left with the retirement home. Sorry, but I figured her son being the second one was a better option than a complete stranger."

"Did you purposely not answer your phone?"

I stop in front of the sliding doors. "Yeah, because that sounds like something I'd do, given the fact I've been her only family for well over ten years."

"You don't understand the ramifications of what she did," my dad snipes.

"Where is she? If you want, I'll take it from here. I'd hate for you to be put out." I walk through the hospital doors, but he's right on my heels.

The nurse's eyes bulge—probably because my dad and I have the same big build that tends to shock people at times.

"Oh no, because now your mother is sitting with her, and I can see she feels guilty, which means this little stunt is putting a thorn in my side."

My dad leads the way to my grandma's room while his words leave me clenching my fists.

"My assumption is I didn't have a signal when they called."

"I'm sure they must have left a voice mail."

"Maybe so, but a notification didn't show up on my phone when I got a signal. Trust me, if I'd gotten the call or voice mail, I would've come without having them bother you."

"I told you years ago if you want to continue a relationship fine, but don't pressure me to."

"No one is pressuring you, but she's only getting older. What if she'd died tonight? Wouldn't you have regrets? I mean, you really can't just forgive her?"

Our voices are growing louder, and when my mom comes out of a room with the look of disapproval at both of us, I assume we were even louder than I thought.

"You two need to stop it. You heard the doctor, stress will only hurt her more. Rex, straighten up and don't blame Noah. We had no choice but to come."

My dad blows out a breath and glares at me out of the corner of his eye.

I walk into the hospital room and find my grandma lying on the bed with her eyes closed. Her dark-rimmed glasses sit on the nightstand. Holy shit, the fact she's only getting older strikes me like a branding iron. I hate not seeing her full of life, or piss and vinegar, as she puts it.

"What happened?" I ask, staring at her monitor as though any of the information on there means anything to me.

My mom and dad look at one another, and my dad rolls his eyes. "A guy named Isaac called 9-1-1. I guess he and your grandma..."

I nod. "Got it."

"Yeah." My mom sits down and crosses her legs, holding my grandma's hand.

"Noah's here, let's go." Dad nods toward the door.

I huff.

"We're not going anywhere. Let's just wait until she wakes up." My mom's other hand pats the top of Grandma's hand. "So, Noah. Were you with a girl?"

"No, I was on an excursion."

My mom's lips turn downward.

"Sorry to disappoint you," I add.

"You're not. I just thought you were distracted somehow." Her eyebrows waggle.

I groan. "This family talks about sex too much."

"Your grandma always said it wasn't anything to hide. Everyone has needs." My mom diverts her attention from me back to my grandma.

It's so weird to be in the same room as my grandma and my parents. It's been so long since it happened. I hate that it took my grandma having a heart attack to make it happen.

My dad picks up a brochure and starts reading it. Would it kill him to show a little concern for my grandma?

Grandma moves a bit, and I stand to make sure she sees me first.

"Glasses," she says in a weak voice. I put her glasses on her face, making her look more like the strong woman I've known my entire life. "Better."

"How are you?" I pat her hand.

She looks around. "Ursula? Rex?"

My dad doesn't stand, but my mom does. "Yes, Midge. It's us."

"You didn't have to come."

"Technically, we did, because Noah was too busy to answer his phone." My dad doesn't look up from the brochure.

"Oh," my grandma says, and her disappointment is clear. She's always wanted a relationship with them. They were the ones who cut her off after she sold the business.

"Regardless, we're all here now. Do you remember anything?" Mom asks.

"No." She shakes her head. "Where were you?" she asks me. "With a girl? At SunBay Inn?"

"SunBay Inn?" My mom looks at me.

Grandma turns to my mom. "There's a girl there. A Greene girl. Noah's been rumored to spend some time with her."

How the hell did she get wind of that? Although it didn't help that a few months ago, she called me to pick up some drunk guy at a bar and drive him home. I was with Mandi that day and she walked over to Truth or Dare with me.

"Really?" My mom's interest perks up.

"She's really cute. I'm friends with her stepgrandma."

My mom and grandma seem to be getting along. My dad scowls from his chair, but there's hope inside me for the first time in over a decade. I need to do whatever it takes to keep this progress going.

"So maybe there will be grandchildren in my future after all?" Mom says with a huge smile.

"Doubtful," I answer.

"She comes from a big family. I'm sure she would want a big family of her own."

I raise my hand. "Can we talk about Grandma's health now, please and stop worrying about me?"

"I'd like to meet her sometime," my mom says.

I roll my eyes, but then I consider that for once, tension isn't filling the room. Well, besides the tension coming from my dad, but if my mom and grandma started to talk again, surely he'd come around. We could put this family feud to rest and I wouldn't be pulled apart in the middle.

"Well..." I tighten my hand around my neck and squeeze. The idea inside my head is probably the last thing I should do.

"Maybe we'll have a wedding to plan soon," Grandma says. "Wouldn't that be fun, Ursula?"

My mom's entire face lights up. "Oh, a wedding."

And that's all it takes for the words to fly out of my mouth. "I'm engaged."

Grandma struggles to sit up, and the brochure in my dad's hands cascades to the floor.

My mom stares at me as though I just said I'd secretly gone to med school and become a doctor. "What?"

"Well, I haven't officially asked her yet." Not a lie. "But I was going to... tonight... until all of this." Okay, total lie.

"Is it Mandi Greene?" Grandma asks.

"Yes." It's a bald-faced lie, but I would never take it back after seeing excitement fill her entire face.

"Do you think she'll say yes?" my mom asks.

"Um... I hope so." Which I really do hope, since I just put us in this situation that I have to figure a way to get us out of at some point.

"How exciting! You go. We'll stay here and take care of your grandma. Go ask the woman you love to be yours." My mom shoos me with her hand.

"We're staying?" my dad says and throws up his hands.

I bend and kiss Grandma's cheek. "You okay if I leave?"

"Go!"

"Thanks." I say goodbye and leave the hospital room.

It isn't until I'm driving back toward the inn that what I did really sets in.

Chapter Ten

Mandi

I'm such an idiot. Why did I ever let him see this side of me? I'm fully capable of solving my problems without any help from Noah. And now, I have to wait up until he returns to check him in and give him his room key. I wonder what made him leave in such a rush. The question was on the tip of my tongue, but I reminded myself that he owes me no explanations. It's none of my business where he has to venture off to, and it's none of his that my business is slowly failing.

I go upstairs to the staff room to change into my pajamas, and when I get downstairs, he's at the door, knocking. I could've left it unlocked, but I don't like the idea of anyone being able to come in while all the guests are sleeping, and all the rooms use manual keys. I haven't had the funds to switch over to a fob system.

"I'm so sorry." I hurriedly open it.

His eyes roam over me like hot fudge over ice cream and my insides melt. "No, I'm sorry for all this trouble."

"No trouble. Do you still have your room key?"

He nods, but his gaze doesn't stop dipping to my cleavage in my silk button-up top. "I do."

"Okay then. I'll just lock up behind you." I slide past him, but he barely moves, so my nipples brush against his bicep. You'd think I stuck them in an electrical socket the way I jerk back as a million volts go off in my body. "Good night, Noah. I'll see you in the morning."

I rush toward the staircase, but he catches my wrist right before my foot lands on the first one.

"Wait." His voice is low and missing its usual confidence.

I slowly turn and tilt my head. He doesn't release my wrist, and I don't pull away. His touch feels good tonight after such a shitty day.

"Can we talk?"

"I don't want to discuss what's happening with the inn. You can't save my business."

He's silent for a moment, so I pull my wrist from his hand and circle back around to take the stairs.

"I have a proposition for you." His voice is stronger now, more how I'm used to hearing it.

Oh god, is he going to ask me to have sex with him? Because I'm not sure I can deny him tonight. All I want to do is walk into those huge arms and have them squeeze me as he tells me things will be okay.

"What?"

"I need you to hear me out. Can we sit?" He signals toward the dining room.

"What exactly are you propositioning me about?" I walk into the dining room, my curiosity too piqued to turn him down without hearing him out.

He takes a deep breath. "My grandma had a heart attack tonight."

I instantly whip around, my hand over my heart. "I'm so sorry. Why didn't you tell me before you left?"

His big hands steady me by my upper arms. "She's okay. It was a minor one, I guess. The hospital couldn't get a hold of me, so they called the second number on the emergency list, which is my dad's."

"Oh. And he went?"

He nods. "He did, not happily, but when I got there, my mom was holding my grandma's hand. I haven't seen them in the same room together in over a decade, let alone touching one another in a caring manner."

I give him a soft smile. "That must've been nice."

He doesn't fully smile, walking past me and taking my hand, leading us to a table near the window. "There's more."

"Okay."

He pulls out a chair for me to sit down and tucks it in behind me. He groans when he pulls out his own chair, folding himself into it. Then he stares at me for an uncomfortable beat. "I hate putting you in this position, and I want you to know you can say no, but I also want you to hear me out."

"Okkaayy." My hands fiddle in my lap. I have no idea where he's going.

"You need help drawing more people to the inn, right?"

I nod.

"I could help with publicizing your business," he says. "I could do some killer brochures, give you a great online presence with a website people can book directly on rather than having to call in. The pictures that I would take alone will spotlight this inn as the best place to stay in Alaska, I promise you that."

"Noah, I appreciate the offer, but we've been over this—"

He's quick to cut me off. "I need a favor in return. I'd be doing you a favor in exchange for one of my own."

"Things don't work like that here. What do you need?"

He chuckles. "So, it's okay for you to do me a favor, but you won't let me do one for you?"

I'm silent for a moment. I never thought about it like that. How I'm so quick to help others but will never accept help myself. "Yeah, pretty much." I cringe.

He smirks, shaking his head. "Not with me. I do that for you, and you do me the favor of..."

I have not one clue what he could be about to ask me. "What do you need?"

"A wife."

My gaze scours his face for some sort of humor. Any minute he's going to laugh and say he's joking, he just needs me to hold some of his things here in storage or something.

Finally, when he continues staring at me, waiting to say something, my eyes widen, and my mouth drops open. "A wife?"

He grabs my hands and holds them together in his. "It's crazy, I know, but my grandma and my mom had one thing in common tonight and that was being overly invested in my love life, or lack thereof, and wanting to know why I hadn't settled down yet. And they were so close, smiling at one another, and I thought if I got married, it would only make them closer. I just sort of blurted it out."

"And when we call off the engagement, then what happens? Or are you thinking we'll actually get married?" I can't believe I'm asking questions as if I'd actually agree to this farce.

"I think we'll have to get married—but only for a year or something. I'll be working still so I'll be gone probably nine months of the year and then we'll divorce with both of us saying it's too hard with my traveling. You could be the one to file for separation, of course."

"Boy, you've thought of everything."

"On the way over, I tried to get the logistics down, so I'd have some answers for you."

I nod, slowly wrapping my head around the information. "Why me?"

"Honestly, you were the first name that came to my mind."

"What an endorsement for love." I press my lips together.

He chuckles. "I don't mean it like that. We've developed a great friendship over these past few years, and I think this could be a mutually beneficial arrangement. Also, if you want any help renovating, I'm your guy."

"So you're gonna stick around town until we plan a wedding, or am I to do it all by myself while you're working?"

He quickly shakes his head as though he's afraid I'm going to say no. "No, I usually take commissioned jobs during the summer months, so I'm available as long as we make this quick. I figure since I already told my family—"

"You already told your family?" I screech, then quiet my voice. "I haven't even agreed."

"I told you, I just blurted it out."

"Oh yeah, my name was the first one in your head, so I get the pleasure of becoming your blushing bride, I forgot. And if I say no, do you have a second pick?" I have no idea why I'm being this snarky. Noah is a good guy, but this is a crazy idea.

He sighs. "It's not like that. Please just think about it."

"How soon are you thinking this wedding has to happen?"

He cringes. "In two months?"

"Seriously? You want me to put together a believable wedding in two months?"

"I'll be here to help."

"And what do I tell my family?" My stomach clenches at the thought of lying to them.

He tightens his fingers on mine and holds my gaze. "That we've slowly fallen for one another over the past few years that I've been coming to the inn, and we crossed some lines and fell in love. I asked you to marry me and you agreed. Make it sound like a crazy love story, and I'm the crazy one pushing the idea. I don't care."

"And what happens after we're married?"

He shrugs. "We'll live together like a married couple but honestly, I won't be around that much, so you'll only have to deal with me for a week or two here and there. We can even live at your place if you want so you don't have to move out once we file for divorce."

I stare at our hands, his big ones covering my smaller ones. I hate everything this represents. Lying to my family and friends is not something I ever do. "I don't know."

"Think about it and let me know tomorrow."

I'm not usually a deep thinker. I always go with my gut. And unfortunately, Noah is right. I need help getting this inn back in demand. I heard rumors that Wyatt Whitmore, the previous owner of Glacier Pointe before he sold it to his son, is looking to buy in the area and everyone seems to want his spas and high-class stay over my intimate and cozy feel. But there are two types of tourists in this world, and I need to find mine.

The last thing I want is for my family to worry about me. They'd probably pool a bunch of money from their own successful businesses and try to save me. Or worse, do a fundraiser. No, I can't let my burdens become theirs.

"I don't have to think about it." I steel myself against the nerves coursing through my body.

"You don't? Are you sure? You might see the benefit of it tomorrow that you don't right now."

I shake my head and chuckle. "I'll marry you, Noah."

His entire face lights up. "Really?"

I nod and he drops my hands, falling to his knees in front of me. The fact I'm wearing a silk pajama shirt and short set and that his face is practically between my legs sends a startling, hedonistic image to the forefront of my mind.

"But it doesn't come with benefits," I add in a rush, in case he's picturing the same thing. The last thing I need is for this to get even more complicated than it already is.

He shakes his head and his gaze locks with mine. "No, but we might have to kiss in front of our families?"

I grin because he's more than likely right and I have no idea how I'll keep things platonic then. "Well, they shouldn't expect that until the wedding. We have eight weeks to plan the wedding, which isn't a lot of time."

"I'll get started on something to help the inn first thing tomorrow."

"Very few people could convince me to do something so irrational, you know." I stand from the chair, and he gets to his feet.

A serious expression crosses his face. "I want you to know how much this means to me. I'm indebted to you forever." He pulls me in for a hug and at first I tense, but then I relax into it, enjoying the warmth of his body and the safe feeling in his arms. He pulls away, resting his hands on my shoulders. "This is the first time I've had any hope that my family will finally come back together. I know that them having to be together for all the events leading up to the wedding is going to mend some bridges. This means the world to me. Thank you, Mandi."

The kicker is that I probably would've agreed to the whole thing without him even helping me around here, because I can see how much it means to him.

I remember those early years after my parents' divorce, being stuck between my dad and my mom. How he'd call and say horrific things about my mom and Hank that no teenager should have to listen to. And the jerk and tug of him asking us to go down to live with him in Arizona and my mom finally having to step in and say no. The legal battles he threatened. The fact that Noah's been in the middle for over ten years has to be grueling.

"You're welcome, and thank you for helping me."

We leave the dining room and walk up the stairs to the rooms and he stops at his door. "Get some sleep, soon-to-be Mrs. Winters, because tomorrow, we go ring shopping."

"Oh, Noah, that's not necessary."

He tucks one strand of my red hair behind my ear and his gaze dips to my cleavage one last time. "It's very necessary. Everyone is gonna know that my wife is mine."

I feel my cheeks heat and I take a step so that my back hits the wall. This isn't how I ever thought things would go with Noah. I really hope pretending to be married to him doesn't break me forever.

"See you in the morning." He winks and I give him an awkward nod, then head down the hall to my room.

It's all I can do to open my door, and when I do, I collapse onto the bed, wanting to scream. I really just agreed to pretend marry someone like right out of some rom-com movie. How is this real life?

Chapter Eleven

Mandi

Present day...

One by one, almost every car belonging to my family members pulls into the parking lot of SunBay Inn, but I'm still being hugged by Midge.

"Welcome to the family," she mumbles into my breasts. She steps back after an uncomfortable minute. "When Noah told me, it made me so happy."

I smile down at her. "I'm glad."

"And then you told no one in your own family?" Ethel says with raised gray eyebrows. "How could you not tell us?"

"That's exactly my question." My mom puts her hand on her hip, staring at me as though knives are about to be thrown from her eyes. She holds up the wedding invitation in indignation. "How does a mother have to find out this way?"

"They weren't supposed to go out yet. Noah and I were going to stop by."

The truth is, I've been dragging my feet for two weeks. Maybe it's good that the printer messed up and sent them out early. My family is going to see right through this charade Noah and I have going on. Who would ever believe that I would marry someone on a whim?

"I'm just going to say it." Posey pushes her way through the group, her very pregnant belly leading the way. "Way to go, sis." She wraps me in a hug and sways me back and forth. "He's gorgeous, you're beautiful, and the two of you are going to look awesome together." She draws back. "He does have a personality, right?"

"Of course he does," Midge answers before me, looking offended the question was even asked.

"Who am I to judge? I married a complete stranger in Vegas." Nikki comes over and hugs me. "Congratulations, but you've put us in a big pickle to get everything planned out. And I'm going to be nice and not mention that I told you years ago you could not marry him."

I roll my eyes playfully. "Thanks, guys," I say, truly thankful for my sisters.

"Years ago?" my mom asks, looking between us.

Chevelle joins the four of us, hugging me too. "I never saw it in you, but I totally love this wild side of you. I think we can all agree it sounds like something I'd do."

"We all know you're waiting on Cam," Posey says.

Everyone quiets.

"I do not like Cam." Chevelle looks disgusted.

"That's not how it seemed in Hawaii," Nikki says with a raised eyebrow.

Chevelle shakes her head and rolls her eyes.

"Have you told your father?" My mom's question is quiet.

I frown. "I would never tell him before you."

She nods, but the fact she asked reconfirms why I'm doing this for Noah. That tug and pull between people you love. Although I hate the type of person my father is, I still love him because he's my dad. I don't think the love a parent has for a child goes away because they didn't turn out the way you thought they would. Same goes the opposite way.

"Where is this mystery..." My mom reads the invitation. "Noah Winters?"

"He's out taking pictures somewhere," I answer because we don't really tell each other everything we're doing day to day. In fact, most of the time, we're separate from one another. Now that both families know, we'll have to change that.

"Pictures?" my mom asks. "Mandi?"

The guilt for keeping so much from her feels like acid on my skin. She's never even met the man I said I would marry. This whole thing was easier in theory than reality.

I raise my hands. "I'm sorry some of you didn't know."

"And others did?" Ethel glares at Midge.

"How about we plan a dinner so Noah can meet everyone at the same time?" I smile, trying to sell the idea.

"And we'll invite the Winters as well," my mom adds.

"Why? They already knew," Ethel sneers.

"Ethel." My mom sighs. "We will come together as a family." Although I still see the disappointment in her eyes, she hugs me. "Congratulations, honey."

Tears threaten to prick my eyes, but I manage to hold them back. I watch as my mom walks back to her car, gets in, and drives away. I've never felt like a shittier daughter.

"We need to make a list of what has to be done for the wedding," Ethel says.

"Who are your bridesmaids?" Chevelle asks.

"Small or large wedding?" Posey asks, rubbing her belly.

"Noah would make a great ring bearer," Nikki chimes in.

"Noah is the groom," Midge says.

Nikki's nostrils flare and her fists clench at her sides.

"Let me talk with Mom again. Maybe at the dinner we can go over everything we need help with. Right now, I have to get back to work. Thank you all for your congratulations."

I hug everyone again and go back to the reception area inside.

Sitting down, I exhale a big breath, closing my eyes and continue a breathing exercise I used to do when I was a teenager after we moved back to Sunrise Bay and I was stressed out. How and when did my life get so complicated?

The uneasiness inside me tells me what I need to do. Mom deserves the respect of meeting Noah on her own, without all the rest of the family. So I dial her number.

"Hello?"

"Hey, Mom, how about you come over to the inn tonight for dinner? I'll invite Noah so you and Hank can meet him?"

"Oh, are you sure? I'd hate to put you out."

My head rocks back and I squeeze my eyes closed. "You're not putting us out. I was afraid to tell you. That's why you haven't met him. I thought you'd think it was a rash decision."

She doesn't say anything for a little bit. "It is quick, but I trust your judgment, Mandi. You've never given me reason not to."

I bite back the bile racing up my throat. "Thanks for that. I'm sorry though. I feel horrible."

"Thank you for the apology, honey. I look forward to meeting Noah tonight. Let's say six?"

"Perfect. See you then."

We hang up and the door to the inn opens, Noah walking through it. "Why are the grandmas outside?"

"Turns out our wedding invitations went out already. Everyone got one."

His eyes widen. "But—"

"Don't worry about that. The secret's out, so guess what you get to do tonight?" I feign excitement. "You get to meet your almost-in-laws." I smack on the fakest smile I can muster.

Noah appears unbothered by this news. He leans his forearms on the counter. "Oh, I can't wait to meet them."

"And there's going to be a big family dinner soon. People are asking questions and I think we need to be on the same page."

"Do I need flashcards to get to know you?"

I shake my head. "No, but we had invitations made without telling anyone we're getting married, so we need to have some idea of the wedding we want."

BY THE TIME my mom and Hank are due to meet us at the inn's restaurant, I feel as though Noah and I are on the same wavelength. We want the wedding to be small, intimate, with no bridesmaids or groomsmen. Just us, with both our families, here at the inn. No huge show or extravagant expense for something that isn't real to begin with.

Noah and I are seated outside when Mom and Hank walk out onto the patio. We both stand to greet them. I always thought of Hank as tall, but compared to Noah, he looks like a shrimp.

"Hank. Mom. This is Noah. Noah. This is my mom, Marla, and my stepdad, Hank."

Mom shakes Noah's big hand and examines him with a narrowed gaze. Oh great, she's already caught on to our charade. "I know you."

Noah nods and my stomach sinks.

"Last summer. You were taking pictures downtown. Do you remember us?" she asks.

Hank intercedes and shakes Noah's hand. "Good to meet

you properly this time and not when my wife is bombarding you about romance."

"Nice to meet you too." Noah takes his time shaking Hank's hand.

Hank hugs me. "How's my favorite innkeeper?"

"She's good." I smile at him.

"She should be great, what with a wedding on the horizon." He draws back and peers at me as though he knows the truth.

Oh jeez, I'm never going to be able to pull this off.

"Well, this was the daughter I'd wanted to set you up with. What a coincidence." Mom gestures at me.

"That is a coincidence." Noah gives her the full wattage of his smile.

"Let's sit." I step back over to my seat.

Hank pulls out my mom's chair and Noah does the same for me. No one except Noah looks at the menu. The three of us know the menu by heart.

My new hire, Matty—a teenager who is still getting used to serving—comes over with shaky hands to take our orders.

"Don't be intimidated by us, we're nobodies," Mom says to the poor kid and places her hand on his.

"Miss Mandi is my boss," Matty says, his cheeks flushing.

"And she's sweet as sugar. Would never hurt a fly," Hank chimes in as if we're some good Southern family.

We all give Matty our orders and he nods about one hundred times, jotting down everything, then disappears back inside the building.

"So, I'm surprised to hear you're engaged to my daughter." My mom turns her attention directly on Noah, who is seated beside her. "When I talked to you, you said you didn't have time for love. That you travel too much."

Noah reaches over the table and grabs my hand. I really wish my stomach would stop reacting like this is real when he touches me. "Well, like you said, that all changed when Mandi and I got to know one another."

"And what a coincidence that you're Midge Winters' grandson?" Hank says. "We've known Midge a long time."

"So how long have you both known each other?" Mom looks down at where Noah's hand is on mine.

I quickly interlock our fingers. "He's been coming to the inn for a little over three years."

"You've been hiding him for three years?" My mom's eyes bulge out and she glances at Hank in disbelief.

"No. We just recently started dating, but with his traveling, it was hard. But then Noah asked me to marry him, and I accepted." That sounds truthful, right?

Matty comes by with fresh bread and our drinks. My wine couldn't come soon enough.

"Thanks, Matty. Good job."

He smiles at me, although his nerves still seem like they're on high alert. I'm right there with him.

"You'll excuse my surprise, Noah. Mandi isn't really an impulsive person. Usually she brings me pro and con lists for important decisions."

I laugh. "Mom, I'm not going to do a pro and con list on whether I should marry Noah. Besides, even if I weigh both sides, I never regret it when I go with my gut."

Noah chuckles. "I do love Mandi's decision-making skills. Especially when they work in my favor." He smiles at me and I tightly grin back.

"Well, should we get to the plans then?" My mom stops her line of questioning that I thought for sure would last the entire dinner. As if we'd be on the quiz show or something while she pummeled us with questions to prove how well we know each other. She pulls out a notebook that says "Our Wedding" on the front.

"What is that, Mom?"

"It's for us to make sure we don't miss a single detail. I figure we only have two months. We need to get a jump on things, stay organized. First of all, how many bridesmaids are you having? Don't worry, Noah, our sons will fill in for you if you don't have enough groomsmen." She puts her pen on the paper. "Nikki, Posey, Chevelle... do you want the sisters-in-law included as well? How about Trina? Anyone from the inn?"

"Mom, we decided that we aren't going to have bridesmaids or groomsmen."

Her pen drops to the table, and she studies us for a moment. "Why not?"

I shrug. "We just want a small affair, here at the inn. Francois can cook the meal."

She frowns. "Oh. Your sisters will be disappointed. What's three bridesmaids and three groomsmen? That's nothing. And—"

"Didn't you two have a small wedding?" I bring it up so maybe she'll let this go. But I always knew she'd want to be überinvolved in my wedding because, unlike Nikki and Posey, I'll allow her free rein. And Chevelle always says she's miles away from wanting to get married. Ever since Hank's illness, my mom acts as though we're all living on borrowed time.

Mom gives me that look from across the table. The one I always give in to. Then Noah looks at me, silently pleading with me not to falter in our decision. But she's my mom and she's the one person on earth I never want to disappoint. And the fact that I'm lying to her only makes me feel worse.

So I cave. "Yeah, I'm sure three on each side would be fine."

"It would?" Noah asks.

I smile at him and nod. "Yeah, it's not so bad."

To my surprise, he smiles and squeezes my hand. "Okay."

"Okay?" Mom beams. "On to the next order of business, how many people are you inviting?"

And just like that, I realize my mom's excitement to plan this wedding has put her on cloud nine. God, it's going to suck if she ever finds out this was all make-believe.

Chapter Twelve

"Okay, I'll admit it. You were right... this time."
—Mandi

Noah

There's a knock on my door right before I'm about to leave the inn with Mandi to go over to her parents' house. They've agreed to host her family and mine with a barbeque.

I open the door, and without even saying hello, Mandi hands me a stack of notecards. "We need to do a quick quiz before we're sent to the wolves."

"Quick quiz? Well, Miss Greene, I didn't think there would be a pop quiz today and I'm afraid I'm very unprepared."

She laughs and starts remaking my bed since I declined maid service.

"Stop making the bed," I say.

She raises her hands and blows out a breath. She looks pretty in a sundress that accentuates her breasts. She's wearing her red hair down and wavy, making me imagine it laid out on my pillow after I've already taken her a couple of times in a night. "I'm so nervous. I swear my sisters will see through this scam when they spend time with us."

I take her hands. Her ring glistens even in the dim light because she takes great care of it. "They won't see through any of it. We just need to be affectionate. You have to be comfortable with my arm around you, with me taking your hand and kissing you." I wanted to broach the subject before, but I didn't want her to think too hard about it, stress too hard about it.

"Kissing?" Her hazel eyes widen.

"Well, we're going to get married, and this isn't the eighteenth century, Mandi." I chuckle.

She nods and stares out the window for a second. "Yeah, that makes sense. So what? Do you want to practice?"

I laugh and look at the notecards on the edge of the bed. Picking them up, I flip through them. "Well, I do think that me really kissing you and you not being uncomfortable is more important than me knowing your favorite ice cream flavor."

"I'm a sherbet girl. Rainbow."

I can't fight my grin. I go sit next to her on the bed. "Mine's chocolate chip."

"That's good to know." She nods. I can tell she's nervous.

"In case your family ever takes us to an ice cream shop, you mean?"

She giggles and her tongue slides out to wet her bottom lip. "You never know when the question might come up."

I cradle her face. "Mandi?"

"Uh-huh?" She swallows hard.

"I'm going to kiss you now."

"Okay," she whispers.

Our eyes meet and I lean forward, taking my time. The second my lips touch hers, my body only desires more. More of whatever she'll give me. I press my lips to hers, unsure if I should slide my tongue between her pouty lips. Would that be too far? After all, I don't think Mandi nor myself are ones for public displays of affection.

I draw back before I push her further than she'd want to go.

"You good?" I ask.

She nods and touches her lips. "Yeah." Her voice is breathy, and I can't help the male pride that has me wanting to puff out my chest.

"So now when I have to kiss you, you won't go stiff because my lips have already been on yours." I smile and rise from the bed.

She does too but grabs the notecards. "Let's just go over some of these on the way."

"I'd rather get to know you the old-fashioned way."

"Well, we don't have time to do it the old-fashioned way."

We walk out of my room, and I lock it before going downstairs.

"So, my favorite board game is The Game of Life," she says over her shoulder.

"The Game of Life? Did you purposely spin to get more kids?"

She glances back as we descend the stairs and I strip my eyes away from her ass. "No. But I somehow ended up there. Even after I always paid for college instead of going right to career."

"I was the career guy."

"And in real life? Did you go to college?"

We both stop our conversation to say goodbye to Trina, who's manning the desk.

Once we're outside and reach my truck, I open the door for her. "I took some classes at a community college, had a great mentor I worked under. What about you?"

"I went to college. Graduated and came back home."

"And how did you get the inn?" I ask once I climb into the driver's seat and start the truck.

"It was going under, and my biological dad gave me the

money it would've cost to send me to school for the fourth year of college. I purchased the property, and here I am."

Her ambition and self-sufficiency are impressive. She intimidates me sometimes. I know what I'm doing with a camera but sometimes I feel like maybe I just got lucky with a few pictures that garnered attention from magazines.

"Speaking of the inn, let's start on the web design and brochure stuff. Want to get started on that tomorrow?" I ask so she knows I'm a man of my word. "And we can go over anything you want done at the inn. I'm handier than I look." I wink at her.

"Hank can help too. He's back to work now."

"Great. We'll figure it out." I pull into the driveway of her parents' house and find us at the end of a very long, steep driveway lined with cars. Anxiety makes all my muscles tense. They're all here for us, because they think we're in love and getting married because of it. Then I spot my mom and dad's car and all the reasons I'm doing this rush back to me.

"You ready?" Mandi asks.

"As ready as I'll ever be."

We both get out of the truck, and I take her hand while we walk up the driveway.

"I'm going to warn you, my mom set up a whole newlywed game for my sister when she married Logan Stone in Vegas. So I put nothing past her. For your sake, I hope she doesn't do some kind of 'how well do you know Mandi Greene?' game, because those notecards are in the truck, and you don't know anything about me."

I chuckle as we approach the door. "Oh, I know a lot about you. Maybe not all your favorites, but I can hold my own. Can you say the same?" I raise my eyebrows and the door opens before she can respond.

"The happy couple has finally arrived. Did you get lost in all the bedrooms over at the inn?" A young woman with long blonde hair, who I assume is either Mandi's sister or stepsister, laughs and steps out of the way for us to enter.

Here goes nothing.

MANDI and I say hello to everyone, and I mean *everyone* because I think her entire family is here. My parents are on the couch, talking with Ethel and Dori, but my dad keeps looking around at Mandi's family members. My dad is an only child, as am I. Even when my family still all got along, there were only five of us around the table.

But here there are kids running around, babies crying, bickering between siblings, laughter among the sisters... I love it.

I bring Mandi over to introduce her to my parents. I'd rather have taken her to their house for a small dinner, but this came first, so here we are.

"Mom. Dad. This is Mandi." I put my arm around her waist as I'm introducing her. She slides into my hold, a perfect fit.

"It's so nice to meet you," Mandi says, and my parents stand from the sofa.

"Mandi, this is my dad, Rex, and my mom, Ursula."

They all shake hands, and we stand there for an uncomfortable moment.

"Do you need help with the wedding stuff?" my mom asks.

"Um... I'm sure my mom has most of it taken care of, but of course we want you included. She's infamous for putting together meetings, so I'll let you know when we have one." Mandi smiles. "Have you been introduced to everyone?"

"Most, I believe. It's a very big family." My mom cringes. "We're not used to it."

"I understand. I mean, I'm used to it, but it can be a lot." Mandi widens her eyes, and my mom cracks a smile. "How about you come with me, and I'll introduce you to whoever you haven't met yet?" Mandi turns to me. "You'll be okay?"

"Yeah, I'll be fine." I give her a smile.

She walks off with my mom, which leaves me with my dad.

"You found the house okay?" I ask.

"Yeah."

"Good." I nod, not sure what else to say.

He looks around. "So you wanna tell me what the hell is going on?"

"I'm not sure I understand what you're asking." I look away from him at everyone else, not wanting to make direct eye contact with my dad.

"You're marrying this Greene girl out of the blue. Did your grandma put you up to this? I swear she faked that heart attack."

I whip my head in his direction. "She did not. They said it was minor and the stent will help her. She's good as new now."

Which really is amazing to me and I'm so grateful.

"You should see it as a second chance to have her in your life again, make amends. Honestly, is the money this important to you?" My jaw is clenched hard, upset we're even having this conversation—again. My mom and grandma have started to open up to each other again. Why can't he do the same?

"It's not the money. And I wasn't talking about your

grandma, I was talking about this marriage thing. Where did it even come from? You've always said you weren't going to get married."

"And Mandi made me change my mind. I've been dropping in at her inn for a few years and got to know her well enough that I wanted to see more of her. And then after a while, I asked her to marry me, and she accepted." None of that is technically a lie. My attraction to Mandi was immediate and her personality drew me back to her every chance I got.

"Well, then I wish you luck, but don't go thinking this wedding will mend fences between me and your grandma. I see you got your mom all invested, but I'm not going to be."

We both look toward the kitchen where Mandi, Mom, and Marla are laughing with the little Noah.

"Well, I'll be sure to keep that in mind."

Hank comes over, and after a while, I leave him with my dad. Not sure an artist and a carpenter have a lot in common, but I don't want to stand next to Dad anymore or hear his negative talk. He's the whole reason I'm doing this, and I can only hope that as the weeks roll on, he'll soften his stance.

As the night progresses, people volunteer to take over one task or another for us, there's talk of who will and won't be invited and the moms talk about taking Mandi dress shopping. For the first time tonight, Mandi's face lights up. I can see how that's something any woman looks forward to.

After we've all eaten and we're outside and hanging around the pool, the clinking of glasses commences. I'm chatting with Mandi, and we look around to see all eyes on us, silverware clinking crystal.

"Kiss her," my grandma says and motions to the two of us.

I place my cup down, and just like in the hotel room, I press my lips to hers in a gentle yet driven way. She meets me more than halfway, and soon I have her completely in my arms. I'm a moment away from my tongue sliding into her mouth when the clinking stops, and I finish the kiss.

Damn, it would've been so easy to let myself go with that kiss.

"Told you we practiced the right thing before coming tonight," I mumble in her ear.

She inhales deeply. "Okay, I'll admit it. You were right... this time."

We both laugh, and when I strip my gaze off of Mandi, I notice everyone is still staring at us. Their expressions make me think that maybe we need to up our game a little more.

Mandi

I've never been that into fashion. Mostly because I live in Alaska and there aren't a lot of stores up here, let alone ones specific to plus-size clothing. Almost all of my clothes are bought online. I try them on and return them through the mail, which is an annoyingly long process. Sure, I can go to a box store, but if I want something more than a basic T-shirt, shorts, or jeans, I have no options. And the boutique stores in our small downtown don't carry anything plus-size.

But I'm getting married, which means dress shopping. My mom, my sisters, and Noah's mom all meet at the dress shop in Anchorage. The minute we enter, all the nerves I had about being here disappear. I've been in other shops that don't cater to plus-size women, and the salesladies give me a look of disdain, as though I have some nerve even being in their shop. And I'll admit, I expected a bit of that today. But I've never felt so welcomed in a clothing store.

The woman I booked a last-minute appointment with, Brena, greets us at the door.

"You must be Mandi?" She looks at me in the middle of everyone. "I'm here to make sure you pick the dress of your dreams." She quickly turns to everyone. "I'm going to steal our bride away. My assistant, Thad, will escort the rest of you ladies to the waiting area. Please enjoy some refreshments while you wait."

Brena and I are just about out of earshot when the doors of the store open.

"You hoo, we're here!" I recognize Ethel's voice. "Where's the champagne?"

"Are they with you?" Brena asks.

I nod. "It's my grandma and her kooky friends. I apologize in advance for anything they might say or do."

She pats me on the back and picks up her walkie-talkie on her hip. "Thad, more of the Greene party and guests up front." Smiling at me, she pats me on the small of the back again. "Let's get started. I need to know all your likes and dislikes. I set five dress styles in your fitting room. We'll try each one on before you even go out and show everyone else. That way you can decide which style you like best, and we'll go from there. I mean, if you want to show your family these five we can, but in my experience, that's how a bride ends up with a dress she doesn't love. Too many opinions flying around. Too much pressure."

"I love you, Brena. Can you shop with me all the time?"

She laughs and takes the first dress off the hanger. "Go ahead and change into the corset. I promise I'm not looking."

I do as she instructs, and I realize that I've never even stood in front of my sisters in only my underwear and a bra before, but Brena doesn't make me feel self-conscious in the least.

As she situates the gown on the floor for me to step into, I fear for a second that she may have underestimated my size. That I'll be trying to pull the beautiful, beaded dress up my curves to no avail. But it slides easily over my hips, stomach, and breasts. If anything, it's a little too big.

"I love your red hair down, but for this dress and neck-line, you should definitely put it up. Do you mind?" She puts my hair in a twist as if she's a fairy godmother and anchors the dress to fit my body with a big clip in the back. I can actually breathe as I stand in the mirror and stare at myself in a wedding dress. "This is another reason I don't allow guests. A bride should only be concerned about her feelings when staring into the mirror wearing a wedding gown for the first time."

As I soak it in, Brena asks me questions about what I like about it, how I feel with it on my body. And we do the same process four more times.

"Okay, now that you've picked the style you love, we're going to go grab a bunch for you. Welcome to the fun part." She does a little clap before she disappears, giving Thad orders of which dresses to pull.

My phone dings in my purse and I take it out.

> Noah: Thank you for taking my mom. She told me she was really excited. I think tux shopping wouldn't have been the same to her.

> You're welcome. She's the mother of the groom after all.

> Still. Just know it means a lot to me that you'd do that. Dinner tonight?

> Sure. But turns out this is quite the process, hopefully I'll be done by then.

> I'd wait all night for you. ;)

The winky face makes my stomach flip.

Brena and Thad return, and I put on a champagne-colored dress that has a beaded bodice with a small belt and puffy skirt. I love the way the neckline dips into my cleavage, and I wonder if Noah's eyes will stray to that area on our wedding day.

My hope that they do tells me I need to get my feelings in check and remember that this is a fake marriage.

We walk out of the changing area, and I can hear all of my guests being way louder than is polite. When I walk into the waiting area, everyone stops and stares. My skin, already flushed from trying on so many heavy dresses, heats further.

"Oh, Mandi," my mom coos while she steps closer. "It's beautiful. You're beautiful."

"I do love the champagne color," Chevelle says.

"Your skin tone goes with it perfectly," Posey adds.

"I just love it," Nikki says.

"I know I don't know your taste well, Mandi, but the dress suits you," Ursula says with a kind smile.

"I couldn't agree more," Midge says from where she stands next to Ursula. I smile, because I'm doing all this for them. "I love that you aren't wearing white."

"Your grandson took my granddaughter's virginity?" Ethel looks at Midge. "That's why she's not wearing white, isn't it?"

"I don't think people go by that anymore, Grandma," Chevelle says.

I hold up my hand. "Enough with the accusations, and no, Noah did not take my virginity." Seriously, they act like I was some old maid until Noah came along.

"Although watching the two of you kiss was intimate enough. I swear I saw tongue," Nikki says.

"Oh please, you and Logan used to go to second base with us in the room. You guys were disgusting." Chevelle pretends she's sticking her finger down her throat.

"Which is how baby Noah came along so fast." Posey laughs.

"Says you. At least I was married." Nikki narrows her eyes at our sister.

"Stop it, girls." Mom looks at Ursula. "I'm sorry about this."

Ursula only smiles and waves my mom off.

"Okay, I'm not completely sold on the champagne color, but jeez, guys. Cool it." I give them all a look I hope makes it clear that they need to be on their best behavior with Noah's mom here.

"Yes, this is just option one," Brena says. "Now we'll go try on option two."

I make my way back to the changing room and hear Nikki and Posey bickering some more while Dori asks for more champagne.

Ethel asks Midge if she thinks Noah might hurt me on the wedding night. "He's so tall and big," she says.

"You're crazy if you think they haven't done it yet," Chevelle says. I can practically see her rolling her eyes.

Normally she'd be right, but I haven't had sex with Noah. Now that Ethel brings it up, I bet he is pretty big... like, everywhere.

"Not everyone is as free as you, Chevelle," my mom says.

"Midge is. That's why I love her."

"Oh, thanks, Chevelle." Midge's voice is warm.

And then I'm in the changing room and, thank goodness, away from the drama.

The second dress is more lace than beads and it covers my entire torso, but it's sleeveless. It's a little more classic and prudish, but it is beautiful, and I do love the white.

When I rejoin the group, the girls are looking at bridesmaid dresses in the corner of the shop.

"What color are we wearing?" Posey asks.

I walk up to the pedestal. "I don't have one in mind yet."

"Well, you have to figure it out," my mom says. "We need to make sure it goes with the table linens and napkins and—"

"Can we please focus on me and the wedding dress?" I'm a little exasperated at this point.

"Yes!" They all hurry back over and stand around me.

"Yeah, no," Chevelle says. "You look... not like you. Too closed off or something."

"I like the other one," Nikki says.

"Does the other one come in white?" Posey asks.

"Too much lace," Ethel says.

I look at Brena through the mirror. "Okay, we'll be back with option number three."

On the way back to the changing room, Brena shakes her head at me.

"What?" I ask.

"I don't know how you brides with big families do it. When I get married, I'm picking one person to come with me, and it'll probably be my fiancé." She laughs. "Or Thad."

We laugh, and I slide out of dress option two into dress option three, which is a white mermaid style but also has a long skirt that wraps around. It's not champagne nor is it white, but maybe off-white.

The minute I step out, Ethel groans. "Another nonwhite dress?"

"I love it," Ursula says. "Really shows off that figure my son loves so much." She winks at me through the mirror, and I see the resemblance to Noah right away.

"I agree with Ursula, sweetie. I think I like this one the best," my mom says.

"Agreed," all three of my sisters say in unison.

I stare at myself in the mirror a little more. Brena gives me a veil to wear, pulling the entire look together. Oh my god, I'm going to marry a practical stranger. Deep breaths. Deep breaths.

"Do you think this might be it?" Brena whispers to me.

"I do. I never thought I'd love my figure as much as I do in this dress."

"It definitely flatters you," she says.

"Sold then." I nod and give her a big smile.

I go back and change into my own clothes, and she sets me up with an alteration appointment to make sure the dress will be ready for the wedding since it's short notice.

"I look good in black," Chevelle says.

"But I look best in green," Posey says. "And since redheads are harder to find something that works for, I say we go with my color. You're both blondes, and green will flatter you guys as well."

"No way. Let's do something bold, like red," Nikki says.

Each of them has a dress pulled off the rack and is holding it up to them. Posey looks funny because her large belly protrudes so much the fabric flows over it.

"Mandi?" they all ask in unison, looking at me.

"You can each have your way. We'll do no specific color," Dori says. "In my day, it was done all the time."

"Red, green, and black?" I raise an eyebrow. "Those are colors for a flag, not an array of bridesmaids."

"This way everyone gets their own style and color, and they can wear it again," Dori says, then walks over to the short dress Chevelle has in her hands. "Did you see this price? We could do them for you. Our sewing club at the Northern Lights is amazing."

"Really? That would save some money," Chevelle says.

I understand where she's coming from. While Nikki

married a millionaire, pro-MMA fighter and Posey married a childhood actor worth millions, Chevelle and I are both single and putting everything we have into our businesses.

I shrug. "Sure, if you think they could get them done on time."

Dori waves me off. "I wouldn't have suggested it if they couldn't. They'll love it."

"Okay, but let's decide on one design and one color," I say.

After a few rounds, I decide it's easier to just let every bridesmaid choose the dress style they like and I take a picture of the dresses and the color we ultimately decide on and send it to Dori's phone.

"Oh, selfie time!" Midge holds up her phone and snaps a picture. "I'll tag Greta and Hilde so they can get started."

"You have Instagram?" Posey asks Midge, looking at Midge's phone.

"She never uses it," Dori says, a tinge of jealousy in her tone—maybe because Midge was able to figure it out and she wasn't.

"I do too. I use it to keep up with Noah." Midge sticks out her tongue.

My three sisters bury their heads in their phones, obviously about to cyberstalk my fake fiancé.

"Why doesn't..." Nikki says.

"He have any pictures of you?" Posey finishes.

"Yeah, you need to be his girl on here," Chevelle says as my sisters all look at me.

"There are no pictures of the two of you?" Ethel comes around Chevelle and looks at her phone. "Anywhere."

"He wants to keep it professional. Who am I to argue?" I answer the only way I can, although I feel as if I'm in the middle of the highway and staring at a set of headlights coming my way.

Dori's eyes bulge. "You better get on that Instagram feed before someone else thinks he's available."

"My son would never let his interest wander. I'm sure Mandi's right and he just wants to keep his private life private."

All their eyes are on me and I suddenly want to send him a picture to post.

I decide to lie through my teeth. "He has another private Instagram account. That's just his business one."

"I'm sorry to usher you all out, but my next client is coming in shortly," Brena interrupts, and I could kiss her.

Now I have a new mission. A new Instagram account for him, selling the image of the happy betrothed couple.

Noah

Mandi walks into my room unannounced. "How good are you at Photoshop and tell me you have another Instagram account that's private."

I'm in the middle of mocking up her new website, making it all romantic and whimsical. Her previous site was way too bland and businesslike, so I'm hoping she'll like the direction I'm going.

"Um? Hello, fiancée."

She flops down on the bed.

"Did you get a dress?" I turn around in my chair.

She nods.

"And do you love it?"

"I do," she mumbles into the comforter.

"Okay... so what's this about a private Instagram account?"

She turns her head and stares at me for a beat. "Did you know your grandma follows you on Instagram?"

I shrug. "Yeah."

"And did you happen to see a handful of new people follow you today?"

"I haven't been on it."

"Well, Midge took a selfie at the bridal store. I guess she has, like, thirteen thousand followers or something. How that's even possible I don't know, but what matters is that everyone was asking why there are no pictures of me on your Instagram."

Shit, that's something one of us should have thought about, but honestly, I don't do a ton on my socials. "I never even thought about our social media."

"Yeah, well, you need to make another account because I said you had a private one, and unless you can Photoshop me into some pictures, we need to take some together."

I lean back and link my hands on the back of my head. "I am good with Photoshop, but what am I going to do, Photoshop you into a picture with a wolf? It's not like I'm posting selfies on there."

"We really didn't think of all the areas people would look at. You should've seen my sisters staring at me. And Ethel was all inquisitive to why—" Her pitch is getting higher and higher.

"Okay, we can do damage control." I turn back around to my computer, open up a new tab, and start a new Instagram account. "First step, done." I pick up my camera and turn around fast, snapping a picture of Mandi on my bed. "Second step, done."

She quickly moves her head into the comforter, blocking her face from me. For some reason, it spurs me to take more photos. I can't deny that I've wanted to take her picture for a while. Her smile lights up a room. I want to see if I can capture that in a picture.

"Come on, look up for me." I get down on my knees, crawl over to the bed, and rest the camera on the mattress. "You said we needed pictures, and since I'm a photographer, there would be a lot more of you than us or me."

She peeks up and I snap the picture before she can turn away.

"You're gorgeous. Stop turning away from the camera."

She lifts her head, her elbow propped up and her hand holding her head up. "I'm kind of camera shy."

"You shouldn't be." I snap a few more pictures of her. Her long red hair cascades behind one shoulder, acting as a veil on the other side of her head.

"Just so you know, we will need ones of you too."

"Want me to set up my tripod? We can do a few on the bed?" I waggle my eyebrows at her. Which spurs a laugh out of her and a cameraworthy photo, so I click my shutter without knowing if it's even in focus. I don't dare take my eyes off hers. "Can I ask you a question?"

"Sure."

"Do you ever wonder if we're going to get too close? If our attraction to each other won't stay locked away in a box?"

"What attraction?"

She's trying to act clueless, but I know she's not. The way her body moves closer to mine without her doing it on purpose, how she reacts when I'm near, there's no doubt we have sexual tension. And right now, my dick is begging me to unleash some on her.

I give her an expression I hope conveys that she's insane for trying to deny it.

She laughs again, this time her head falling back until she's unsteady and falls onto her back. Her shirt hugs her breasts and it's all I can do not to keep looking to see if I can tell where her nipples are. God, what I would do right now if she was mine to climb on top of and seduce.

"I'm serious," I say. "You have no idea how much you're driving me crazy right now."

A flush creeps up her neck, the one I loved seeing when

I'd arrive late at night. As if she was surprised and not expecting me, but pleased.

I snap a couple more pictures.

She sits up, crosses her legs, and places her hands in her lap. "Noah, you know we can't do anything. We're committed to this fake engagement."

"Exactly. So it's not like we can sleep with other people. We might as well sleep with each other." The idea that's been rolling around in my head for the past few days sails past my lips.

She slides off the bed. "You're insane. Then feelings will form, and lines will blur, and we'll end up hating one another in the end when one of us makes the mistake of thinking this is real. If we keep clear of anything sexual, we'll get through this. Your mom and grandma were really getting along today. It's a great sign that they're making progress."

Now if only my dad could get on board.

Mandi makes sense and I don't ever want her to hate me, so I set aside my stupid idea, even though a huge part of me knows the two of us would be fireworks in the bedroom.

"That's great to hear. Come over here. I want to show you something." I forget the camera for a moment and tuck my half-chub dick away where he belongs. "I still have to get a few more pictures, but I had a friend do a new logo for you. What do you think?"

I hold the chair out for her. She clicks through the pictures, checking out the different pages on the website. The logo isn't as masculine as it once was. The colors are now light and flirty, pinks, golds, and light gray.

"I love it," she murmurs, her gaze bouncing from one side of the screen to the next. "Does this mean I have to get everything outside redone too? Make it all match? Brochures and things like that."

I can see her worry, but that's the last thing I want. "Let's not get ahead of ourselves. Just tell me if you want anything changed on the site."

She continues to flip from page to page. "No, it's amazing. Truly. I love it."

Her smile is thanks enough. I would have happily done this without her agreeing to marry me.

"Good. Then I'll get all that going. And let's go have dinner tonight and talk about what else you want to do. How we can really drive people in here."

"This is enough, Noah, honestly. This and all the pictures you're taking, the brochure you're going to do... I can't take any more."

I sit on the edge of the bed and stretch my legs. She watches me with interest. "You're legally marrying me knowing we're going to divorce a year later. I'd say that's going above and beyond. In order to pay you back properly, I'd need to tear down the entire inn and rebuild it."

"You would not." She stands.

I get up to follow because all I want right now is to be with her. "Dinner?"

She laughs. "It's not even dinnertime yet."

"Surely there are other wedding things to do? We need to find a bakery."

"Francois can bake the cake."

We leave my room and I shut the door. "There's something about a guy named Frank baking your wedding cake." I shudder. "What about that bakery in Lake Starlight?"

She shakes her head. "Never going to have availability on this short notice."

"It doesn't hurt to try. Come on. Let's take a ride."

She descends the stairs, and at the bottom, we see Frank with his hands on his hips. "You two. Now." He nods toward the dining room, then turns and walks in that direction.

"He heard you call him Frank," she whispers.

"You're aware you shouldn't be afraid of your own employee, right?" I follow her through the inn to the dining room.

"I'm not afraid. It just makes it easier if everyone calls him Francois."

We follow him into the kitchen, where he stands in front of a sheet of paper on the counter with Mandi's handwriting on it. He slides the paper over to us and I see that the top reads "Wedding Menu" in her girly handwriting. The woman is organized.

"I didn't know we made a menu."

Mandi looks back at me. "I didn't think you cared."

Frank blows out a breath and slides the menu in front of her. "This is all... ew. Mostaccioli , fried chicken. It's not a barbeque, Amanda, this is your wedding."

She sighs. "We were doing it family style, and those dishes are the easiest. Why would we have you go to so much trouble when it's just going to be a small event?" She slides the menu back to him.

"Because you only get married once. And your food should speak to you both. It should be dishes you love. The entire dining experience should say amour. I cannot do that with noodles and sauce. And what are these pigs in a blanket?"

"I do love pigs in a blanket," I say behind her, and she looks over her shoulder and smiles at me.

"I was just trying to make it easier on you. Feel free to make whatever you want." Mandi turns to leave, but Frank pulls her back by her elbow.

"Again, this is the bride and groom's decision, not the chef's."

Mandi looks at me. "What's your favorite food?"

"You do not know your groom's favorite food?" Frank asks in that annoying French accent.

"Favorite fancy food then," she says.

"I love steak."

Mandi nods and turns to Frank. "Steak then. A potato and a vegetable. We'll do soup and salad to start."

"So now we've gone from a barbeque to home-on-the-range cowboy dinner."

She throws her arms in the air. "You're the chef. What do you want to prepare?"

I've never seen Mandi raise her voice at anyone. I wonder if all the pressure and lying about the wedding is getting to her.

Frank looks at the ceiling as if he's praying for help. Either that or patience. "How about filet mignon with garlic butter melted on top. A puff pastry filled with chicken wrapped with spinach, cream cheese, and herbs. Not just mashed potatoes but twice-baked potatoes. Asparagus wrapped with bacon. We'll do our most popular soup of chicken and wild rice, followed up with a garden salad with a homemade dressing. Not much I can do there."

"Substitute the dressing with one of my mom's and that all sounds great," Mandi says with a nod as though it's decided.

"Sounds amazing. My stomach wants a trial right now." I rub my belly.

Frank laughs and pats my stomach. "In good time, big man."

"And cake for dessert," Mandi adds.

"No cake for dessert. No one wants cake for dessert. I

make chocolate soufflés and a tray of macarons for each table."

"That's a lot of work."

"For a wedding? No. You need to demand more. This is your special day, Amanda."

She grins. Frank is right—we can't be doing everything half-ass because this isn't a real wedding. We need to make this wedding like the one we'd want if this was for real.

"And we can have pigs in a blanket for an appetizer?" I ask.

"Little sausages wrapped in pastry?" His nose wrinkles.

"Francois?" Mandi says with a lilt to her voice as if to say he's the groom and it's what he wants.

"I'll find some way to fancy them up," he grumbles.

"Great. Thank you." Mandi leaves the kitchen.

I'm about to follow when Frank stops me.

"You know, Noah, that a lady should never sacrifice. The man who loves her should make sure she gets what she wants. If you truly love her, you won't allow her to skimp on her own enjoyment." He raises both eyebrows.

I feel as if I'm stuck in a game of Clue and people keep eyeing me suspiciously as though I'm the murderer.

When I make it outside of the kitchen, Mandi is talking to a couple. I slide in next to her.

"Hello, I'm Noah, Mandi's fiancé." I put my hand out.

The woman looks shocked, inspecting Mandi's left hand immediately. They congratulate us both.

I allow them to have some small talk before extracting Mandi from the conversation. "If you'll excuse us, we have a cake tasting to get to."

We say our goodbyes, but once we're in the office, Mandi doesn't grab her purse. "Francois is making desserts."

"We need a cake to cut. Every wedding has a cake to cut.

Plus, I'm pretty sure you'll be ready to shove it in my face by then."

She laughs. "It's a was—"

I place my finger on her lips. "It's not a waste. It's our wedding." I lower my voice to a whisper. "Fake or not, we're going all out. Do you understand? Now, I'm going to drive you over to Lake Starlight, and if she can't fit us in, I'm going to offer to pay double." She opens her mouth, but I shake my head. "You are going to have everything you want. No more arguments, okay?"

She nods.

"And you do not make decisions without me like that menu you made, okay?"

She nods.

"Good. Now let's go."

I take her hand and we walk out of SunBay Inn. I'm determined to make this the dream wedding Mandi always wanted—real or not.

Chapter Fifteen

Mandi

Noah comes down from his room and stands in front of the reception desk where I'm going through the day's checkouts.

"Hey, I gotta head out for two days this week. There's a waterfall I need to shoot for a magazine. How about you come with me?" Noah leans on the counter and pins me with a stare.

"I can't leave the inn."

He looks around, probably thinking what I already know —that there aren't nearly enough people around with it being tourist season. A good sign of things not going as planned.

"Can't Trina help you out? It's two days."

"Where are you going? I'm not really an outdoorsy person." Though the thought of some alone time with Noah isn't exactly a deterrent.

"I'll be there to protect you." He wiggles his eyebrows a few times and I can't help but smile.

I'm really realizing what he meant by the whole sexual tension thing. The other day, he was coming out of his room and putting on a shirt at the same time. His back is rippled with muscles, and all I could think of for six hours after that was what it would feel like to rake my fingers down his back.

I cross my arms and tilt my head. "Cabin or tent?"

"What fun is a cabin? A tent. You'll fall asleep to the sound of the waterfall." His expression says he thinks it'll be awesome. "Come on. I want you to get a glimpse into my life."

My heart rate picks up. "Why?"

He bites his bottom lip. "I just want you to see why I love it."

"When are you going?" I look at the small desk calendar I keep on the counter.

"End of the week. Wednesday through Friday. We'll be home before the weekend rush here, and I'll even help you clean rooms when I get back."

I roll my eyes, although it's in that playful, flirty vibe that Noah's been pulling out of me lately.

"What do I need to bring?" Although I'm agreeing, there's a whine in my voice because even though I want to spend time with him, I know it's a horrible decision. We should try to keep our distance as best we can.

"Just clothes. I've got everything else we'll need."

"Okay. Hey, while I have you, I'm heading over to the grandmas' this afternoon to check on bridesmaids' dresses. If you wanted to see Midge, you could join me…"

He shrugs. "Sure."

"I want to be there by one."

"Want to have lunch before?"

Every time we have to do anything wedding related, he asks to spend a little extra time together. Whether it's lunch or dinner or ice cream the other night. I'm trying not to read too much into it, but I have a feeling we're straying off the path we decided to travel and moving into uncharted territory.

WHEN WE WALK into Northern Lights Retirement Center, I see the eating area is still busy with lunch service.

As soon as we walk in, everyone hits their plastic glasses with their forks. It doesn't really have the same effect as clinking glasses, but I stop and glance back at Noah. He's smiling as though he's happy about this development. I begin walking again, heading toward Ethel's table, but Noah grabs my hand and tugs me into his body.

He dips me and presses his lips to mine, this time opening his mouth slightly. Enough for me to taste the peppermint he had on the ride over. My insides turn to goo and my stomach explodes like the grand finale of Fourth of July fireworks.

I'm flipped up to stand and he winks to a round of applause from all the seniors.

"Be careful, you might turn them on," I whisper.

"The men were already turned on when you walked in." He slides his hand in mine and leads me over to Ethel's table.

His compliments about my looks are more blatant now and I can't deny that I love them. No one has ever made me feel as wanted or as beautiful as Noah Winters, which is probably a little sad since we're not even a real couple.

"Look at you two, quite the couple," Dori says, but something in her eyes doesn't sit well with me.

I smile at Dori, then turn to Ethel. "I'm here to look at the bridesmaids' dresses."

"Yes, they're pretty much done. The girls are stopping over when they get off work tonight to try them on."

"Sit down, you two. You can have my dessert." Midge places a cup of pudding in front of Noah.

I chuckle, and he holds the chair out for me before folding himself into one of his own.

"That's okay, we ate before we came." He slides the pudding cup back over to Midge.

"Lunch is almost over, then you guys can come down to my room if there's time before the next activity," Midge says.

"Maybe they want to come to mine," Ethel says, seeming offended.

"We can go to both." I have no idea why they're pushing this so hard.

"Mandi, I wanted to let you know that I had the sewing club make a junior bridesmaid's gown as well," Ethel says. "It's in navy blue, like you requested."

"Junior bridesmaid?" I glance at Noah to see if he has any idea what she's talking about, but he shrugs his big shoulders.

"Calista happily agreed to walk down the aisle with Rylan. I guess they have some soccer tournament the day after the wedding, so she's going to spend the night at Marla and Hank's," Dori fills me in on details I wasn't aware of.

"Rylan is standing up too?" I look at Noah, who didn't really care which of my brothers stood up for him at the wedding. He said all of his friends moved out of Greywall as soon as they could, and he isn't inviting anyone from New York because he felt bad asking them to pay for airfare and take time off work for a fake wedding.

"Yes, your mom arranged the whole thing. It will be so cute." Dori looks off into the distance as though she's picturing it.

"Okay great. And then that's it."

"Just Emelia's dress, since she's the flower girl," Ethel says.

"But no ring bearer," I clarify.

"Oh, we're going to have Logan escort little Noah down the aisle," Ethel says.

"Good thing you guys don't need my help planning any of this." My sarcasm is clear.

Noah's hand lands on my thigh, making me jump. His hand hits the table, and he retracts it, shaking it against the pain. Dori's staring at me when I apologize to him for being so jumpy.

"You know what? After lunch today, we're having dance lessons. You two can join us and practice up for your big day." Midge seems very excited about her idea.

I look at Noah. "Oh, well we..."

"LeeAnn! Can Noah and Mandi join us for the dancing lesson?" Midge calls.

LeeAnn, the social director, among many other roles, comes over. "Congratulations, you two. I can't see why not."

"Great," we deadpan at the same time.

Forty-five minutes later, after a lot of help from Noah and me, the tables are pushed back and the chairs are stacked, making room for a dance floor.

A couple in their late forties comes into the room and introduces themselves as the instructors. The woman is wearing short heels and one of those dresses where the fabric flares when she spins, and the man has on high-waisted pants and black shiny shoes.

"They're the real deal," I whisper to Noah.

"I have a confession." He stares at them. "I'm not some closet, good dancer. I didn't even think about our first dance. I might've dipped you earlier, but that's about the extent of my moves."

I look up at him and bite my lip to keep from laughing at how stressed he looks. He's even got a bead of sweat along his hairline.

I link my arm with his. "Don't worry, we can step on each other's feet."

He looks down at me and our eyes meet. "You really are the best."

Our gazes lock until the woman claps loudly. "Okay, everyone. Grab your partner and get out on the dance floor!"

"Come on, you two." Midge waves her hand as she does the box step with Earl, whose eyelids keep drooping as though he might fall asleep.

"No time like the present." I take Noah's hand and drag him onto the dance floor. We might as well make the best of it. His large hand lands on the small of my back and he links our hands between our bodies. "So far you're not that bad."

There are a few slower songs at first, and it takes a little bit of time for me to get comfortable being so close to Noah. The smell of fresh soap mixed with his masculine scent wafts off him and makes me want to move closer even though he keeps his distance between our bodies, concentrating on his feet.

The male instructor comes over and positions our bodies so they're closer, more like a couple. He shows us the steps and asks Noah to borrow me for a moment to show them with me. Noah eyes him hard as the man spins me away and back. I fall into his chest, unable to keep myself upright. Noah intercepts and takes over, the man waving his arm and telling him to go ahead.

"I guess I really am an amateur," Noah says.

"It's too much pressure with that guy. I prefer dancing with you. Spin me."

He pushes me away. When he pulls me back into him, my hand lands on his hard chest and we both laugh.

"Now I spin you," I say.

The instructor ends up giving us an unimpressed look because neither of us is taking this seriously, but I don't need a smooth dancer. Just someone who likes to have fun no matter what we're doing.

As we grow more comfortable with one another, I wrap my hands behind Noah's neck, and he rests his hands on the small of my back. We sway instead of attempting some fancy dance we don't have the footwork for.

"Close to You" by the Carpenters comes on and I step closer, resting my head on his chest. His arms tighten around me, and for one full song, I enjoy the moment as if it's real. Having Noah these past weeks has proved to me that I could get used to having someone permanent in my life, but the problem is, I only picture Noah there.

His heart beats steadily and I sink into his chest as though I'm six and he's my favorite teddy bear. Noah offers me a stability I've never felt in my life. My parents split when I was young, and after my mom and Hank were married, I remember feeling like I was waiting for the other shoe to drop. For something to happen to ruin their marriage and send Hank on his way.

I look up at Noah for a second as he turns us away from the group. He's watching me. My fingers play with his ponytail, and he bends down. No one is asking us to kiss, so if he kisses me, he's doing it because he wants to. I hate how much I hope for more than a press of his lips. I want his searing tongue in my mouth, to feel how badly he wants what I do.

I rise to my tiptoes, ready to meet him halfway when the song ends and "Do You Love Me?" by The Contours plays. We've gone from slow dance to dirty dance in a matter of seconds. Both of us look around at the group, our mouths hanging open.

"Your grandma…"

He cringes. "I can see."

She's grinding on Earl's thigh, and he looks as if he's struggling not to fall over. I spot another couple where the man has his hands on her hips, grinding his pelvis on the woman's ass while she's bent over.

I blink and blink again. "What just happened?"

"I have no idea. We went from sock hop to orgy." Noah winces and looks away.

"Come on, you two. This is the best kind of dancing." Midge waves at us to get moving.

"Fuck that," Noah murmurs to me.

"I can't not look. Help me."

He covers my eyes with his hands and situates himself behind me. "Lord, please let it end soon."

I take his hands and turn around between his arms. "You know, you're not that bad of a dancer."

"So, you'll still marry me?"

"Just tell me when and where."

He takes my head in his hands, his thumbs running across my cheeks. "Do you ever wish it was different with us? That we would've crossed the line before this whole farce began?"

I cover his hands with mine. "The obstacles would still be there. You'd still be traveling and have your home base in New York, and I'd still be committed to staying in Alaska. But to answer your question. Yes, I see it."

"See what?" He inches closer to me. "Tell me what you see."

I close my eyes. "I see us together. Lazy Sundays in bed, walks along the bay, movie nights together."

"Ah, you see all the things Sunrise Bay offers."

I open my eyes. "What do you see?"

"You with me on excursions. You in a bikini on an exotic beach. Or bundled up with ten layers out in the snow, complaining about how cold it is and me promising to get you warm when we get back to our cabin. The fireplace roaring, hot cocoas in our hands, and you naked in my arms."

"Two very different lives," I say with a frown.

"Yeah, they are." He sounds pained when he says it.

This wedding better come quickly so he can go on an excursion and we can get some distance from one another, otherwise I'm going to fall into bed with the man. Or worse, in love.

Noah

"I look like a giant blueberry!" Posey shouts, looking down at her dress that cuts off under her boobs and flows out over her swollen belly. "I'm sorry, Mandi, but I'm going to have to forbid any pictures of me in this thing."

"You look beautiful," Mandi tells her sister.

I sit on a table in the back of the sewing room that doesn't look all that used. Shouldn't there be a lot of thread or sewing machines in here?

I was disappointed when the dancing ended. I almost kissed her. God, I wanted to so badly. If it wasn't for the dirty dancing starting, I would've. The urge to taste her is way too strong.

I don't know why I asked her to go on an excursion with me. Maybe to try to prove to myself that my lifestyle isn't for her. I have no clue, but she's coming, so I'm going to have to deal with blue balls for two days straight.

"Watch Noah for me?" Nikki walks her kid over to me and he just stares.

"Sure." I look at the kid. "We share a name."

"Me Noah!" He points at himself.

I nod and put on a placating smile. "Yeah, I'm Noah too."

"Me. Noah!" He points at me. "You. No Noah!"

I chuckle. "You can call me whatever you want, buddy."

Nikki comes out wearing a dress that has multiple layers of see-through navy fabric that's meant to flare out when she spins. "What is this?"

Mandi bites her lip.

Chevelle waddles around like a penguin, looking for scissors. Her dress goes down to her ankles and doesn't flare out enough, so she can't walk properly. "I need scissors! I don't wear anything past the knee, Grandma."

"This is a wedding, not a dance club, Chevelle," Dori tells her.

But Chevelle searches every surface anyway.

Mandi glances across the room at me, biting her lip.

"Sorry," I mouth.

She shrugs.

Meanwhile, baby Noah's eyes are on me, giving me his worst death glare. I guess at almost three, it's the best he can do.

"Listen, girls, you asked for the sewing circle to make the dresses, so you're going to wear them. It's one day," Mandi says.

"And a lifetime of photographic evidence." Posey puts her arms over her belly.

"Plus side. We'll always remember how much bigger you were than me when you delivered." Nikki laughs, touching Posey's stomach.

Posey picks up Nikki's hand and drops it. "I heard you show faster the second time around." She eyes Nikki's stomach.

"What?" Mandi asks, her mouth dropping open. "You're pregnant?"

Nikki's lips tense into a thin line as she glares in Posey's direction. "I wasn't telling anyone."

"Since when do you keep these things from us?" Chevelle waddles over to the group.

If I wasn't cornered by baby Noah and on babysitting duty, I'd leave them to their discussion. I'm not even sure I'm supposed to see the bridesmaids' dresses, or maybe it's only the wedding gown. That thought makes me wonder what dress Mandi picked out. Of course, it's not like I'll be peeling it off her body on our wedding night. No honeymoon. Fuck, that sucks.

"Since I didn't want to rain on Mandi's day or time." Nikki narrows her eyes at Posey.

"I see where you get it, kid," I say to baby Noah.

"It's okay. I'm happy for you." Mandi smiles at her older sister.

Everyone else offers their congratulations and hugs Nikki.

"Good, while we're sharing the good news, I wanted to let you all know that I'm bringing someone to the wedding." Chevelle smiles wide.

"Who did you meet?" Mandi asks.

"Tell me it's not Cam?" Posey says.

"Of course it's not Cam. That's just a childhood infatuation," Nikki chimes in.

"There's no infatuation with Cam." Chevelle inhales a deep breath and turns her head so her sister can't see her cheeks. When she looks up, our eyes meet, but I try to act unfazed, as though I don't see the truth in her sister's words.

"Anyone else have any other big news?" Mandi asks.

"Anyway, Noah, I wanted to tell you... if you're not moving in with us because of me, I'll have you know I'm a very good roommate." Chevelle stares me down.

"Oh, yeah, as long as you don't mind her taking your clothes out of the dryer before they're dry so she can use it and don't care that she doesn't wipe down the cups after the dishwasher, so they always come out of the cupboard with a little water in the bottom," Posey says to me.

"That does bring up a good question. Why is Noah staying at the inn? He should be with you at the apartment." Nikki looks between the two of us.

"He not Noah!" baby Noah screeches. "Me. Noah."

"Of course, sweetheart," Nikki softens her voice.

"I'm at the inn all the time anyway." Mandi shrugs, trying to play it off.

"But when I went over there the other day, you referenced Noah's room. Wouldn't he just stay with you?" Posey's eyebrows rise.

"What? I don't know. Why are you asking all these questions?"

"I mean, she went for an off-white dress, so it's not like she's saving herself," Dori whispers loudly enough that we all hear her.

"Well, thank you. Noah, did you get that?"

"He not Noah!" Baby Noah screams.

"I think we should go," I say.

Mandi puts up her hand. "No, let's just finish this." She turns to Posey. "Sorry, you're pregnant, but you're my sister and you're in the wedding, looking like a blueberry or not. If you're lucky, maybe you'll have the baby before the wedding and we can alter the dress." Then she turns to Nikki. "Yes, you might look like a flapper girl, but it flatters your figure, so deal with it. And lastly, Chevelle..." She picks up a pair of scissors from a nearby table and hands them to her. "Have at it. Is everyone happy now? Thank you all for making this so easy on me. As if there isn't enough stress with planning a last-minute wedding."

Mandi stomps out of the room. I slide off the table,

picking up Noah, who I swear tries to kick me in the nuts. I hand him to Nikki, then run after Mandi, who's already at my truck by the time I reach her.

"Hey, you okay?" I click the key fob and she opens the door.

"I'm fine. It's just all too much."

I start the truck and we both buckle up. "Tell me where you want to go."

"Go toward the mountains. There's a ledge that looks over the bay that I go to a lot."

I follow her directions, and we end up on a rock ledge near the top of one of the mountains that looks out over the bay. After she gets out of the car, she screams at the top of her lungs, her fists clenched, her mouth wide open as she lets her frustration boil over.

I lean back and watch her, loving that she's letting me see this side of her. The one that doesn't have it all together. The one that gets as nutty as the rest of us. And damn if I don't want to fuck her more than ever right now. This whole display has provided me with a new fantasy—one where we're fighting one minute and our mouths are smashed together, clothes ripped off the next.

Her head falls back, and she stares at the sky. "I'm sorry. You shouldn't have to see this."

I approach her and stand beside her. "I feel guilty for asking you to go along with this fake marriage. It's too much stress, added onto the stress you already had with your business not doing as well as you want."

She sits and crosses her legs. "No, it's just my sisters. It's always something. I mean, I love them and wouldn't change having them for the life of me, but sometimes…"

I sit next to her, stretching my legs out in front of me. "I wouldn't know. But I can tell you, having no one sucks too.

It's my sole responsibility to get my parents to mend their relationship with my grandma. It might be easier, or maybe I'd feel less responsible for making it happen if I had some siblings."

"I know. That's why it's not like I wish I didn't have them. It's just hard in a big family. This is supposed to be my time. I guess I thought they'd push their issues aside. The whole reason I allowed the grandmas to make the dresses was because I know Chevelle doesn't have all the money in the world. And I'm not sure what dress Posey thought would make her look like she has an hourglass figure when she's very pregnant." She picks up a pebble and throws it over the ledge.

I place my hand on her knee. "You guys are lucky to have one another. But they're extra lucky to have you."

She smiles and rests her head on my shoulder for the briefest second as though it's a reprieve for her.

"You can keep it there longer if you'd like."

So she does, and I take the opportunity to kiss the top of her head. Her shampoo smells like pears and honey.

"They have a point," she says. "But I'm not sure what we're going to do about it."

"What do you mean?"

"Us not staying together. I definitely shouldn't be charging you. Do you think they know?"

"Well, we could say we don't want to live together until we're married. That we're being a little old-fashioned and keeping separate residences until we're husband and wife."

She sighs, and I feel the weight of the world in that sigh. "It's hard lying to them."

"I'm sorry." I frown.

She lifts her head and looks at me. "Stop apologizing. I agreed to this. I'm in this."

"But your business hasn't improved yet." I tuck a strand of her hair behind her ear.

"It will. I never would've gotten time to do what you've done so far. It'll all pay off, it just takes time. And once I'm not planning a wedding, I'll come up with some more promotions and things to get me back on track."

"Still. I can't thank you enough. I'll never be able to properly repay you." I wish I could write her a check, but Mandi would never accept that.

"Stop acting like what you're doing isn't enough. We made a deal. And every time I see your mom and your grandma talking, it makes me happy." She stares off into the sky for a moment. "Want to know something?"

"Anything you'll tell me," I say, wishing we could stay here all night.

"It's a truth," she says as though it's a warning.

"Okay."

"Truth is, I probably would've agreed to this fake marriage without you helping the inn in return. If you haven't noticed, I'm kind of a sucker for family and relationships. Even my own dad I gave numerous chances before slowly giving up on our relationship."

"Truth?" I ask.

She nods. "Yeah."

"I never would've allowed you to do it without getting anything in return."

She turns her head and smiles at me. "I know."

We stare out at the sky, shoulder to shoulder.

I pull out my phone. "Turn around." We both turn so our backs are toward the cliff, and I hold up my phone. "Now smile."

She leans in close, her cheek on mine, and I snap a picture.

"For the new Instagram account," I say.

"Oh, good idea. Should we take more?"

"Kiss my cheek?" I say and snap a picture. "Now lean your head on my shoulder." I click another picture.

I take a few more of just her with the beautiful view behind her. Afterward, we take some very cheesy pictures with our hands in the shape of hearts in shadow.

"Truth?" I ask her.

She nods. "Yeah."

"I didn't want those only for Instagram. I wanted to remember this moment. When it's all over and I'm out of your life."

She smiles and takes my phone, sending the pictures to herself. "Me too."

We leave shortly after and head down the mountain to play make-believe. I can't speak for Mandi, but it's becoming harder to continue the charade because I'm pretty sure I'm falling for my fake fiancée.

I take her hand, but her phone ringing interrupts us.

She picks it up and says, "I'm sorry—what? Okay, we're on our way." She hangs up. "Posey's in labor."

I guess I know what my night's going to entail. Family time with the Greenes. The funny thing is, it doesn't sound so bad.

Chapter Seventeen

Mandi

Posey delivers a beautiful baby girl named Shay.

And since she was in labor for the majority of the night, Noah and I left late but head over to the hospital in the morning.

Posey is awake and watching television while Gavin's talking on his cell phone off to the side. Shay is in the bassinet. Not exactly the moment you imagine after someone gives birth.

"I can wait outside," Noah says.

"Don't be silly. Come in and meet your niece."

He does a little blink when I refer to Shay as his niece as though the thought hadn't occurred to him and I feel a pull in my chest, knowing his relationship with this little one won't stand the test of time.

Posey is eating her breakfast and I whisper, trying not to interrupt Gavin, "You look great."

"Thanks! And now I won't be a big blueberry for your wedding. So win-win. Thanks for coming early, little one." She blows a kiss to Shay, who's still fast asleep.

"Not too early, right?" I ask.

"I think maybe they had my date wrong," she whispers. "She's healthy and good, doctor says she can come home tomorrow." She cringes. "We didn't even finish the room in the back of the salon for when I bring her to work."

Gavin hangs up the phone. "Want to hold her?" He picks up Shay and offers her to me.

"I'd love to." He puts her in my arms, and I gaze down at the little beauty. She's perfect.

Noah snaps a picture with his phone, and we exchange a smile.

"For bragging," he says to Posey and Gavin.

"I wanted to talk to you actually," Gavin says to Noah.

I sit in the chair and rock my little niece, unable to stop staring at her red hair and pale skin, just like Posey and me. Her small five fingers wrap around my index finger, and a sense of love and peace rushes through my body.

"We need some headshots for the mayor's office, and I thought you might be able to help us. I know the sheriff's office needs some too."

"Um..." Noah glances at me.

I shrug to say it's up to him. He runs his hand through his hair.

"And Noah, just so you know, it's uncle duty to take newborn pictures of your niece. I know you're used to photographing the wild, but can you brush up on your portrait skills?" Posey pushes away her empty tray.

"Oh yeah, sure. Although it's not really my strength. I don't know if you saw Fisher and Allie's pictures," he says, never one to overpromise. Which makes me think about us. He's always very clear about where we stand.

"I did and those turned out great. I just figure while we have you in town, we might as well take advantage. And of course we'll pay you. I mean, you need the money for the wedding, right?" Posey smiles.

Noah returns her smile, but my assumption is he doesn't need any money.

We spend twenty minutes with them until Posey yawns for the tenth time. I put Shay back in the bassinet and we each say our goodbyes.

"If you call my office, they'll start setting it all up." Gavin hands Noah his card. "Two weeks, guys, and you're husband and wife. How exciting. Now I just need to get this one to walk down the aisle and marry me." He thumbs toward Posey.

"I wasn't going to look like a snowball at our wedding, Gav," Posey says. "You can plan it in three more months."

Gavin looks at Noah. "When are they going to realize they're beautiful in our eyes no matter what?"

Noah turns to me. "I wish I knew." Then he looks back at Gavin. "Congratulations again."

I hug Gavin, and Noah shakes his hand. While we walk down the hallway of the baby wing of the hospital, I wonder if I'll ever be here as a patient. Being engaged to a fake fiancé isn't exactly going to make it happen.

"I have to buy some new camera equipment," Noah says. "I'm a tad worried… I'm not a portrait photographer."

"I'm sure you'll do fine. I mean, Fisher is a hard man to please and they hung a picture right above their couch."

He blows out a breath. "We'll see. I guess if I have to hightail it out of town after the wedding, you'll understand —I took crap pictures."

He laughs, but the mention of him leaving Sunrise Bay leaves a gaping hole in my chest. I cannot imagine him not being here.

"Who knows, maybe you'll enjoy it." I raise my eyebrows.

He shakes his head. "I've never been someone who can sit still for very long."

We walk out to his truck as his words ring in my head. It's crystal clear that there is no future for us, so what am I to do with all these feelings I have for him? Will they go away after he leaves, or in a year when we divorce? I haven't met a man like Noah before, and at this point, I don't think I'll ever meet a second.

THAT WEDNESDAY, I'm going over everything with my staff before Noah and I leave. The fact that I might not have cell service while we're gone is scary, but they handled it when I went to Hawaii. Surely they can handle this.

Noah walks in after packing up the truck and stands idly by as I give all my last-minute instructions.

"Now go." Trina shoos me away with her hand. "Go have a nice getaway before the wedding."

"I'm not sure sleeping in a tent is a nice getaway, but it will be nice not to have to think about wedding plans for two whole days." I glance over my shoulder at Noah, who is standing with his hands shoved in his pockets. "Call me if you need me."

"We will," Trina says. "Now force her to leave, Noah."

He pulls me by the back of my shirt, twists me around, and throws me over his shoulder, fireman style.

"Noah!" I say in shock.

He opens the door of the inn and carries me to the truck. "I fear if I don't take you this way, you'll keep delaying our trip."

"Put me down." I can't help but fear how much I weigh on his shoulder. "This can't be comfortable for you."

"You're nothing. Have you seen my muscles? I kind of like you in this position."

His ass is right at my eye level and I kind of like it too, if I'm being honest.

I realized a long time ago that not every man could carry me like this and having sex with a man holding me up against a wall might be out due to my size. Not that I care, there are plenty of other positions, but I'm not naive to the limitations. But Noah challenges all my assumptions because he handles me with ease.

He drops me to my feet in front of the truck's passenger door. Opening the door, he waves me in. "Your chariot, ma'am."

I pretend to glare at him, although I kind of loved him carrying me like that. "Thank you, but I could've used my two feet."

"Believe me, you'll be on those two feet for most of our hike today." He shuts the door and I raise my hand, but he's rounding the truck.

As soon as the door opens, I say, "Hike?"

He laughs and starts the truck. Looking at me, he reaches across me, takes the seat belt, and straps me in. "How else are we going to be remote for two days? Don't worry, it's beautiful."

"And you're not going to kill me, right? Because in all honesty, you should wait until after we're married. You can have the inn then. Although it doesn't make a ton of money."

He chuckles, pulling out of the parking lot. "The way that mind of your works, Mandi. I fucking love it."

"Is that a compliment?"

He looks at me from the corner of his eye. "Yeah, it's a compliment."

We drive in silence for a few minutes, getting farther away from Sunrise Bay. "Truth?"

"Yeah," he answers and turns down the radio.

"I don't travel a lot. The Hawaii trip was a sort of one-off. Something my family planned. I'm not used to being away from the inn, and I realize now that it's kind of sad that I live in this amazing state and haven't ever really explored it."

"So what you're saying is that you might just be a closet explorer."

I laugh. "Well, I'm pretty sure that when I say explorer, I'm still talking about hotels and cabins, not tents and sleeping under the stars."

He shakes his head. "It's the best. You'll see."

"What? Backpacking?"

"Sleeping under the stars."

"I think you're extremely lucky you haven't been eaten by a bear yet."

He chuckles. "Probably. But what is life without a few risks?" He glances in my direction for a second before returning his attention to the road.

"I'm not a risk-taker. Never have been."

His hand extends over the console between us, and he grips my knee. "I'm not sure that's true."

I scoff. "You go all over the world, stay in the most remote parts all on your own to capture a photo. You've probably been face to face with death more times than you care to tell me. I live in a small town where my entire family is within a stone's throw."

"Mandi, you took over a failing inn. Talk about a risk. You employ people who rely on your business sense for their livelihoods. Those are all risks."

I shrug. "It's not the same. I knew what I was doing when I bought the inn."

"Did you really?" He cocks an eyebrow.

"I suppose not entirely. I learned on the fly."

"And that's taking a risk. Otherwise, you'd be working for someone else right now. But you're your own boss and that's admirable and always a risk. And all that isn't even mentioning you agreeing to my crazy offer of a fake marriage."

I lay my head back on the headrest and think about what he said. Maybe he's right. Sure, I don't take risks physically or with my safety, but maybe I take risks in a different way.

After a few minutes, I turn my head in his direction. "Truth?"

"Yeah."

"You make me feel like a different person." There's a warm sensation in my chest.

"Is that good or bad?" The way he asks the question makes it sound like my answer matters immensely to him.

"Good. You make me feel like I'm some amazing woman capable of anything."

He stops at a traffic light as we drive through another small town and looks at me. I know for a fact this place only has one light. "You are, Mandi. To me, you're the most amazing woman I've ever met."

I shake my head. "You only say that because I'm helping you."

"No." He shakes his head. "I've always thought it. It's how you are with people. The way you treat everyone like they're your best friend and you really care about them. I see the people at the restaurant. Each table is eager to have a few minutes with you. And I know how that feels because it's what I want every day too. To steal a few moments alone with you. I love hearing what's in your head."

I suck in a shallow breath. "Careful, Noah, you might get lucky if you keep talking like that."

He pulls to the side of the road and puts the truck in park. "I meant every word that just came out of my mouth." His eyes hold mine and my heart does this funny thing where it skips a few beats. "Truth?"

"Yeah," I just about whisper.

"I have no idea how I'll ever walk away from you. It will be the hardest thing I've ever had to do."

It's on the tip of my tongue to ask why he has to walk away from me. Maybe we should give this thing a shot for real.

"But I'd only end up breaking your heart. While you're not meant to travel the world, I'm not meant to stay in one town for the rest of my life. I couldn't get out of Greywall fast enough when I was eighteen. It wouldn't be fair to you."

I plaster on a fake smile and nod. "You don't have to clear things up for me."

He puts the truck in drive. "I think we could have a great friendship though."

I huff and stare out the window. "Yeah, definitely," I say, not meaning a word of it.

Chapter Eighteen

Noah

park the truck at the farthest point we can go. We spent the majority of the second half of the drive in silence. Mostly because of my jackass comment about how I'd never stick around and I'd break her heart. Like she's some lovesick puppy dog. If anything, that's me, because I'm the one starved for her attention. But I meant what I said. Walking away from her will be the hardest thing I've ever had to do.

"Okay, I packed your backpack for you. Your water is on the side of the bag. I've got the tent. We're set."

She nods.

We hike for a while until we can hear the falls crashing down on the rocks below. I've been to this waterfall numerous times, so I know this is nothing Mandi can't handle.

The only problem is how quiet she is. I don't like it.

After a mile, I stop us to sit on a rock and take a drink. "What's wrong?"

She shakes her head, but I'm not going to spend the next two days here with her pissed at me and playing mute.

"Listen, I shouldn't have said what I did." I put the cap on my water and place it back in the pocket of my backpack.

"It's the truth though, isn't it?" She looks around at the landscape, at anything but me.

I take out my ponytail and run my hands through my hair to secure it back again. "Well yeah, but—"

She stands. "It's fine, Noah. I get that you probably think I'm sitting here heartbroken, but I'm not. I know the score between us. Let's just get where we need to." She walks back over to the path, and I follow her.

"I like you, Mandi," I continue, knowing I should let it go, but I wanted to bring her here to have fun. To hear her laugh echo through the open space, to be alone with her.

"I like you too, Noah. And like you said, we can be great friends." The sarcasm in her voice is thicker than pudding.

"You're upset."

She stops for a second and whips around to face me. "I'm not upset, okay? Well, no, I am upset, but only because you keep making these comments about what a great person I am. And bringing up the sexual tension between us. Picking me up fireman style and carrying me out of the inn. You're sending mixed signals all over the place."

I stare at her, my chest heaving for a breath, and something in me snaps. "What do you wanna hear? You wanna hear how much I fucking want you? All the time? That not a minute goes by when I'm with you that I don't think of something sexual? But I owe you more than that. I owe you everything if this plan works. And I won't hurt you."

"You seem to think I'm so fragile." She throws up her arms. "If you think because of my size I'm some virgin who can't get a man, think again. I've had plenty of experience in my lifetime and there will be men after you."

She circles back around, but I grab her elbow and twist her back to face me. Then I step forward.

"Because of your size? Damn it, Mandi, when have I ever

made you feel like I judge you about your size? You're the most gorgeous woman I've ever laid my eyes on. I think I've made that pretty clear. If you knew how many times I'm having to think of things like dead puppies and my grandma having sex just so I don't get a hard-on around you, you'd believe me. I don't think of you as some virgin who's never had a man and is grateful for my attention. And the fact that there will be someone after me pisses me the fuck off. Because I wanna be the man. I wanna be the man who can live in a small town with you, raise babies, and sit on a porch watching our grandchildren play. A man who is okay with a simple life, who doesn't thirst for adventure. I wish so badly I was him, you have no idea."

She blows out a breath and stares at me, her eyes full of some emotion I can't pinpoint. "I never want you to be anybody but who you are."

"But I do wish I was different because I don't want to say goodbye to you." I raise my hand and cradle her cheek, my thumb brushing over her lips. "I want to kiss these lips whenever I want. I want you to be mine to touch whenever the mood strikes. I want to know you're mine to be inside of every night."

"I don't know what to say." Her words and her body aren't on the same page. I know because her eyes are begging me to take her.

"I just want you to know where I am with this. That I'm trying to be an upstanding guy here, but that doesn't mean I don't want you. I'm sorry if it feels like mixed signals." I run my thumb over her bottom lip again, knowing I need to pull my hand away.

She steps back and shutters her emotions. I can't get a read on her anymore. "Let's get to the campsite. I'd hate for you to have to put up the tent in the dark."

Circling around, she starts walking and I watch her for a moment before joining her. I'm not sure how much longer my willpower will stay intact. I'm trying desperately to do the right thing, the smart thing, but it feels as if everything will come to a head soon.

Forty minutes later, we make it to the area where I plan to set up camp at the bottom of the falls.

"We're going to stay here?" Mandi asks. "Don't bears go to the river to catch fish?"

I chuckle at her concern. "Yes, but there are bears everywhere. I need to capture a picture right when the sun is lowest."

I drop my backpack, then unpack the tent and put it together.

"I'm not sure about this. Should I have written a goodbye letter to my family? Crap, I don't even have a will. Who will get the inn?"

I shake my head and get the poles for the tent together. "You worry too much. I'll protect you."

"How? I know you're big, but you're not bear size." I hit my chest where my gun sits in my vest, and she gets the message. "Oh. Then I'll be stuck to you like glue."

"Fine by me." I wink.

"If you want to keep things platonic, you need to stop with the winking."

I wink again and she chuckles, her mood lighter now. Thank God, I hate seeing her stressed out or upset. Even more so when I'm the cause.

She stares at the flowing river and the waterfall. "It is beautiful, I'll give you that."

"Amazing what Mother Nature gave us, huh?"

I hammer in the stakes for the tent. When the tent is up,

I lay both of our sleeping bags inside. Then I go to work on the fire.

Mandi sits on a rock, observing quietly. "I have to admit, not wanting to get on the whole sexual tension thing again, but watching you work so hard is kind of a turn-on."

I chuckle. Once the fire is roaring, I grab my camera and sit next to her on the rock. I point the camera at the falls to set up the shots I think will work best.

"What are you doing?"

"I'm cropping out shots, messing with some dials and focus, to get an idea of what picture I want."

We discuss how it works when I get contracted for work —whether the magazines or online companies ask for a certain picture or if I have some artistic license—and I tell her a bit about some of my favorite jobs that I've done. I hand the camera to her, positioning one hand on the focus. I cover her hand with mine and move it around so she can see the difference.

"That's crazy. What I thought was the perfect picture, you only make sharper. Amazing." She clicks the camera, then moves so my hand slides off. Then she turns the camera on me. "Tell me, Mr. Winters, what's it like to be on the other side of the lens?"

I shake my head and hold out my hand.

Snap. The shutter goes off.

"Stop taking pictures of me." I cover my face with my hands.

"Come on. You're sexy." She moves my hand away from my face and squints into the light. She snaps another picture. "I think I like this side of things. I want to be a photographer."

She stands and focuses the camera down on me, continuing to click the button, picture after picture. Then she moves to the trees—but she hears a sound.

I look over and see a small red fox at the edge of the forest. I stand slowly and get up behind her, placing my hands on the camera again. I don't have to look to know what will work for the picture.

I whisper in her ear, "Now, we're going to slowly move the focus in, making things blur around it."

She inhales.

"Take the picture, Mandi," I say quietly.

She does, and when she turns my way, our mouths are only millimeters apart. I swallow, wanting so badly to kiss her.

"It's really cool looking through the lens," she says, eyes still locked with mine. "All the things you barely notice. The camera has a way of making you notice the little things."

I take the camera from her hand and place it on my bag. Then I stand back up and weave my fingers through her hair, pulling her mouth to mine.

"I'm sorry, but I can't resist any longer," I whisper and capture her lips with mine.

I'm not sure if it was the photography talk or being so close to her again, but I can't resist the urge to possess her any longer. I need to taste her.

The second our lips touch, my tongue slides along her parted lips, in desperate need of entry. She opens, and the conversations we had earlier fade into the background the longer our tongues learn how to dance together. She twists, and with a push of my hand on her lower back, she's flush against my body. A strangled moan sounds in her throat and I place my thigh between her legs.

She lightly grinds along on my muscled thigh while her

hands cling to my body, gripping my shirt. My mouth leaves hers only to explore her neck.

"Damn, I knew it. I knew you'd be everything I need." I squeeze her ass, encouraging her to grind along my thigh. My lips travel back up her neck and jaw to her mouth, covering it with my own.

I'll never have enough of her.

"Should we take this to the tent?" she asks when I strip my mouth from hers, my fingers going up under the hem of her T-shirt.

"Probably." I take her hand and lead her to the tent, then unzip it. When I look back, her face is flushed and her lips swollen. "Are you sure you want to do this?"

She crawls in ahead of me. "You don't need to have this conversation. I get the no strings attached thing. I just hope to get you out of my system."

I should want the same, but in the back of my mind, I know there's no working her out of my system. I have a feeling she's going to stick around like a brand on my skin.

She lies down on the sleeping bag and I blink to make sure it's not my imagination. She's still there. I enter the tent, zipping it shut behind me.

I take off her shoes one by one, then her socks, before doing the same for me. Climbing over her body, I feel like a teenage boy again because if I'm not careful, I'm going to embarrass myself and come way too soon. No woman has ever turned me on this much, nor have I waited this long to get what I want.

My lips meet hers again, but this time—maybe because we have the security of the tent—there's no holding back for either of us. Clothes are unbuttoned, unzipped, and stripped, one after another. Soon we're both naked and I'm reaching into my bag for one of the condoms I brought just on the off chance I needed them. I guess I know my willpower pretty well.

I take in her naked flesh, laid bare in front of me. She's stunning. All woman, all curves, sexy as hell.

She gets up on her knees and runs her hands down my chest, taking the condom out of my hand and sliding it down my hard length.

I've wanted this for a long time, and I intend to savor this woman.

Chapter Nineteen

Mandi

Noah is the biggest guy I've ever been with. Just putting on his condom made my pussy clench in anticipation of finally having him inside me, but also wondering if he would fit.

"God, I want you so bad," Noah says, lowering himself over me.

Although I want to straddle him, I refrain for our first time together.

He kisses his way up my body, his mouth molding to my curves. With every other guy, there was still a small piece of me that was self-conscious, but Noah's continued praise of my body and his obvious desire push any negativity far from my mind. He pushes my breasts together and sucks on my nipples one at a time, over and over.

The ache between my thighs intensifies and I spread myself open for him in obvious invitation. I've waited so long, I don't want to wait anymore. He makes his way back down my body, and when he reaches the apex of my thighs, his knuckles run down the length of my outer lips.

"Tell me this is from me." His voice is rough and low when he feels how wet I am.

"God, yes."

He grins and then settles between my thighs. His hot

breath flows over my core and the anticipation of having his mouth on me has me wanting to squirm. When he runs the tip of his tongue over my folds, his eyes glued to mine the entire time, I let out a breathy moan.

I wiggle under him, the ache for release a screaming need inside me already. I clench down to keep my orgasm from erupting. His thumb circles my clit as he draws back, watching me enjoy his hands and tongue on me.

"I love how wet you are. I can't wait to slide inside you. Tell me you want the same."

My back arches off the tent floor. "I do." My words are strangled.

His other hand runs up my body, through the valley of my breasts as I rise and fall from his touch.

"More," I beg.

He chuckles. "More?"

I nod.

He dips his head again and this time he pushes a finger inside me as he sucks on my clit. He twirls his tongue around it and thrusts another finger inside me, arching them to hit my G-spot.

"Noah," I say his name like a prayer and a benediction. "Don't stop."

My body is so reactive to him, I'm squirming and wiggling until he lays his arm over my stomach, forcing me to remain in place. His efforts don't let up. Of course he's exceptional at eating me out. I should've expected nothing less. The cresting of my orgasm is like climbing a ladder that never ends. He keeps pushing me up a notch and then another, to levels I never thought I'd reach. My climax hits me like a bolt of lightning. My back flies off the tent floor, my legs closing, except Noah holds them open, making me ride out the pleasure while he laps at my release.

Finally, my mini convulsions die down and he lifts his head, settling his hips where his head just was.

"I could watch you come all day," he whispers before taking my mouth with his.

Instead of his tongue, it's his cock sliding through my drenched folds. He pushes inside me and stills. It takes me more than a few seconds to adjust to his size.

"Sorry," I whisper.

He kisses my jaw. "Take your time."

"I'm good."

He stretches me more than any other partner has. Every nerve ending is lit up like a Christmas tree. Finally, he moves inside me. Slowly circling his hips, then sliding out and back in. The friction of him inside me only builds the pleasure back up.

"So perfect. I knew we'd be perfect together." He kisses my throat and the soft spot by my ear. "I'll never grow tired of this. I'm not even finished, and I already want you again."

"Harder," I beg, my nails scratching his shoulder blades, needing to anchor myself to him.

"My pleasure." He draws back and thrusts back in me so hard, I slide up on the sleeping bag. He dips his head to take one of my nipples into his mouth.

"Oh god," I pant, holding his head to my breast.

He increases the pace and I bring my legs up to his hips, giving him the ability to get even deeper.

"Don't stop," I beg for the millionth time.

Curses fall out of his mouth, praises about my body, how much I turn him on. And then he details what he's going to do to me for the rest of the trip.

There's no promise of the future beyond these couple of days and I'm okay with that. It's all about getting each other out of our systems. Then maybe all the serious stuff will disappear and we can go back to our simple arrangement.

My second climax comes fast and hard, and I fall over that imaginary cliff. He watches me for a second before his lips fall to mine and his tongue slides inside. The taste of myself on his tongue only turns me on more. Noah doesn't stop kissing me with every ounce of passion he has until he tenses and stops thrusting, coming with a low groan.

He kisses me slowly and bites my bottom lip, soothing it with his tongue and sliding it back in my mouth. We lie like that until he grows soft inside me.

"I don't want to leave you," he confesses, withdrawing completely and opening up the tent to dispose of the condom.

I'm not sure what he does with it, but I love that he comes back to me, takes both sleeping bags and zips them together, and we crawl inside. His fingers graze my skin. Eventually the exhaustion of fighting our feelings and the release of the sexual tension get the best of us, and sleep comes.

I CAN TELL that the sky is a little dimmer when I wake, though not dark since it's summer. The spot next to me is empty and I can see the fire blazing outside through the tent walls. I grab my shirt and pants, sans bra and panties, unzip the tent, and crawl out.

Noah's there, snuggled in a sweatshirt with his pants on. It looks like he's preparing something over the fire. He looks back at me over his shoulder and smiles. "You're up."

"You shouldn't have let me sleep that long."

There's a large log next to the fire now and I wonder how

long he's been up. I sit on it and run my hands over my arms.

He stops what he's doing, tears off his sweatshirt, and hands it to me. "Here."

"Oh, I can get—"

"It's fine. I'm warm anyway."

It's not warm per se and it's not cold either, but I run a little on the cold side usually. I put on his sweatshirt that smells just like his soap and I love the way it drapes over me. "Are you making dinner?"

"I am. I caught a fish. You okay with that?"

I nod. "I can't believe you've been so busy while I've been sleeping. I feel incredibly guilty."

He kisses my temple. "Truth?"

"Yeah."

"I like taking care of you. Will you let me?"

I can't help but give him a goofy grin. "Okay. I kind of like you taking care of me too."

He slides closer to me and his free hand slides around my back, rubbing my hip. "So am I out of your system yet?"

"Since I want to straddle you right now? I'd say no."

He chuckles so deep that it echoes through the night air. "Good, because I want to ditch the fish and have you for dinner."

I sigh. "We're in trouble. You realize that, right?"

He laughs again. "I seem to be out of fucks. All I want is to have you over and over again."

"Well then." I strip off his sweatshirt, placing it on the log. I pick up the metal thing he's cooking the fish with and lay it so it's no longer in the flames. Then I straddle his lap. His hands rest on my hips. "Let's delay dinner a bit."

His hard length pressing against my core says he's on board.

I lean in closer, wrapping my arms around his neck. "Truth?"

"Yeah."

"I'm not wearing any underwear."

His fingers inch up the back of my shirt, rounding my rib cage until he pinches my nipples. I suck on his earlobe and moan.

"I thought you might like that," I whisper in his ear.

"Oh, I do. I might just have to stipulate no bra wearing in the future."

I laugh, but he takes the hem of my shirt and raises it up and off my body, placing it on top of his sweatshirt. "You have no idea how long I've wanted to drown myself in your tits." He takes them in his hands, running his thumbs over my nipples, making them into stiff peaks.

"They're all yours."

"Don't tell me that because I'm going to motorboat you, titty fuck you, and constantly grope you if that's the case."

I give him a seductive smile. "All things I'm more than happy to oblige. But first, there's something I've been wanting to do."

I get up from straddling him, open up his jeans, and lower his zipper.

"Fuck, Mandi," he says, rising up off his ass so I can push his pants down to his ankles.

"Surprise! Someone else likes to go commando I see."

His dick points north and I grab the base of it, pumping lightly at first. I can't even wrap my fingers all the way around his girth.

"I wanted easy access. I thought I'd be able to control myself now that I've had you. Turns out that's not possible."

I lower my mouth and suck on the head. He twists my hair around his fist, out of the way so he can watch me. My tongue runs up, teasing him, until my mouth covers his tip again and I swirl my tongue over him. His groan keeps me going.

"Fuck yeah," he pants, his grip pulling harder on my strands.

I bob up and down on him, my hand wrapped around his base, pumping him the entire time. He grows harder in my hand and the saltiness of his precum coats my tongue.

"I'm gonna come," he warns, thrusting his hips so his dick breaches the back of my throat. I don't stop, instead looking up as his eyes close. "You're killing me. You'll be the fucking death of me."

I love the way he talks when he's turned on. As if he has no control over his words when he's about to come.

My other hand fondles his balls and squeezes.

"Shit." His hips move faster, my hand matching his rhythm.

Suddenly he explodes in my mouth, stream after stream filling it while I swallow. When he's done, I lick the tip of his dick clean.

He releases my hair, and it spills along my back.

"You will be rewarded greatly now." He tears my pants off of me and has me bend over the log, ass out.

His head dips between my legs and I'm rewarded with another fireworks-worthy orgasm courtesy of his tongue. After he helps me back up, he's hard again. I wonder if we'll ever get enough of one another, because he goes into his backpack and brings out another condom. I straddle him, sinking down on his length with a moan.

"Make those tits bounce in my face," he says.

Which I do, and I'm surprised neither of us gets a splinter from the friction of our bodies on the wood.

Three orgasms later, I'm still not even close to being

done with him. I stay on him like a koala bear on a tree and he runs his finger up and down my back.

I look at the woods. We're completely alone. "I get it out here. Sex in the wilderness is really great."

He kisses the top of my head. "I know. It's a first for me."

"What?" I lean back and stare at him as though he has to be lying.

"You're the first woman I've ever taken with me on an excursion."

I wrap my arms around his. "Thank you." I squeeze him, and he holds me tightly.

"Come on, let me feed you some real food."

We both laugh, and I put his sweatshirt back on without any pants and he puts on his pants without any shirt. We eat the fish he prepared with a beautiful view of the river and cascading falls.

I guess he really knows how to romance a woman. No matter what happens between us, I'll never forget this moment with Noah. Ever.

# Chapter Twenty

Noah

*W*hen will I ever get enough of this woman? Mandi is nestled in my arms, and we're snug inside the sleeping bag, naked.

"How have things progressed with your dad and Midge?" she asks.

I feel guilty since nothing has progressed on that front and it's the whole reason we're getting married. "They're still not talking. I'm not sure what to do. My mom is coming around, but my dad won't budge."

She turns and lifts herself up on her elbows. "Maybe we need to come up with a plan."

"Like?" I run my fingers down her hair.

"Hmm... a dinner? I could have it after closing hours at the inn. Just your parents, Midge, and us."

"He'll probably leave when he figures out no one else is there."

"We could lock them in a room together." She giggles.

"I'm not sure anything is gonna work. Short of you getting pregnant and us demanding they get it together or they can't see the baby, I'm out of ideas." I finger a lock of her hair again. "I'm not suggesting that as the solution, by the way."

The idea of impregnating Mandi should scare me more than it does.

"Let me think on it a little." She twists around and lies with her back to my front.

"Who is walking you down the aisle?" I ask, trying to get on the topic of her dad without her thinking I'm prying. She hasn't mentioned him at all when we discuss wedding planning.

"Hank. I almost broke and asked my dad, but I couldn't. He's made his bed and I can't pull him back into our lives after he's gotten so many people mad at him."

"What did he do? I mean, you don't have to tell me if you don't want to."

She sits up and faces me. "No, it's fine. After he and my mom divorced, he tried to remain in our lives in his own half-ass way. He was always more concerned with Jed than the rest of us. Thought Jed would get a free ride to college for football and probably go pro. He was doing some things he shouldn't have to try to make that happen, and after Jed found out, he cut Dad off. Nikki tried to let him back into her life, but he used her for Logan's connections. He has a new wife and kids. That's where his interest lies. I haven't even told him I'm getting married."

I frown. "Why not?"

"Because I told myself when he calls me, I'll tell him. And he's yet to call." She shrugs. "So why should he know? Plus, Hank's been more of a father to me than him. Not to mention it's hard to respect your dad when he cut off your mom, who gave up everything for him."

I remember her mentioning that. I figure it's the whole reason I'd never get Mandi to travel with me. It's clearly important to her to provide for herself and be self-sufficient.

If she were following me around the world, all her eggs would be in my basket so to speak.

"How long were they together?" I ask.

She fiddles with her fingers. "Eighteen years, I think. But my mom gave up everything to move to Arizona with him. And when she found out he was cheating on her, she moved us all back up here to her hometown. We lived with my grandparents for a while, and eventually she rekindled things with Hank and found her happily ever after."

"They do seem happy."

She makes a sound of contentment. "Hank was Mom's only real love. My dad was just a stand-in, I think. She'd never tell me that, but I know it's the truth."

"Well, I'm glad she married someone else before Hank because I can't imagine if you weren't in my life. You're the most caring and giving person I've ever known." I probably shouldn't have said that, but it's the truth and I can't keep quiet about it. I want this woman to know how special she is. I wrap my arms around her and entice her to lie back down.

"Thank you. After we moved here, Nikki was boy crazy. Posey was too young. She just wanted to be Mom's protector. But I was Mom's helper. If dinner needed started, I'd do it. The laundry folded, I'd do it. I tried to do things without her asking because I knew she needed the help. After she and Hank got together, Rylan was born, and I just continued helping. Before I knew it, it was the role I took on in the family."

"Which makes you a great innkeeper." I squeeze her against me.

"I suppose, but sometimes, like the other night with the dresses, I want to tell them all off. I just want to do what I want and not give one crap about the consequences."

"I wish I could make that happen for you. Although I can give you a life without being everyone's caregiver, I sense you don't really want it."

She laughs, but it's hollow. "How sick is that? But it's the truth. I don't want to leave them. They're everything to me."

I kiss the top of her head. "You're exceptional."

"Stop putting me on some pedestal. I have plenty of faults."

I laugh now. "Such as?"

"Such as me leaving dirty dishes for Francois every time I cook. The fact I still call him Francois because I'm too much of a people pleaser. But I will say that when we went to Hawaii, I swindled things so that Chevelle had to stay with the grandma gang so I could actually have a vacation without having to take care of all the seniors. I was proud of myself for that."

I laugh hard and she looks at me in surprise. "I'm proud of you. That's awesome."

"Once I got over the guilt, I really did enjoy myself."

"When I found out you were going, I wanted so badly for a contract in Hawaii to call me, so I'd have an excuse to run into you there."

She smiles, and it makes her hazel eyes twinkle. "Really?"

"I'm not sure you understand how attracted I was to you. Still am." I tuck a strand of her red hair behind her ear.

"Same."

The conversation dies and I don't have it in me to bring up our future. I feel so good right now, and I don't want to ruin it.

My eyes are just about to lose the fight with sleep when Mandi whispers my name.

"Yeah?"

"I have to go to the bathroom."

"Okay." I sit up and open the zipper of the tent.

It must be the middle of the night because it's almost full dark, though it will never get there. The embers of the fire are just about out.

I hand her a flashlight and shine it around toward the forest as she slides out of the tent naked. "Not worried about poison ivy, huh?"

"I'm not going into the woods, and I'm not sure what you're doing with that flashlight but you're not going to watch me pee." She snags it out of my hand.

"I was going to make sure you weren't eaten by a bear."

I hear her footsteps along the branches and leaves. Then the stream of pee, but it stops abruptly.

"Noah? I hear something." Her footsteps emerge and the flashlight beams all over the sky and the trees. "Oh my god."

I grab my gun and hop out of the tent. "What is it?"

"Something's out here." She drops the flashlight and runs right into my arms.

I hold her to me and hold the gun out at I have no idea what. It may not be completely dark, but the woods have a darkness all their own.

A flashlight floods our vision and I push Mandi behind me, blocking her view.

"You can't be here," a man says. "If you want to camp, you have to go to the actual campgrounds."

I put down my gun when I see it's the park ranger.

"Adam?" Mandi screeches.

He shines the flashlight at us again. "Oh shit. Come on, you guys. Go get fucking dressed." He turns to his partner. "It's my stepsister and her fiancé. I can't believe this."

"Impressive," his partner says, looking at me and my exposed dick.

"We're never talking about it again," Adam tells him.

We scramble into the tent, and I put away my gun. We dress fully before coming back out. I hold out my documents from *National Geographic* that give me a pass to tent wherever, knowing that I won't abuse the wilderness and will leave it as I found it.

"At least this way, our relationship is believable," I whisper.

"Thank God I was behind you. If my stepbrother saw me naked, I would've died."

We step out of the tent and find Adam and his partner, each leaning against a tree.

"Why are you up in this area?" Mandi asks him. "How did you find us?"

"We followed the animal sounds," his partner deadpans.

"You should be happy it's me." Adam takes the paperwork from my hand. "And I'm taking a few extra shifts because of the adoption."

Mandi smiles. "Oh, when does it go through?"

Adam and his wife, Lucy, are adopting a baby girl who was born addicted to opioids. We had a big discussion about it at the barbeque after I met their adopted son, Trey.

"In a few weeks." Adam hands the paperwork back to me. "I guess you guys are good to stay here then. Let's keep this between us, okay?"

Mandi and I nod, and Adam and his partner leave.

Once they're gone, I take out my camera, happy I didn't fall asleep because the waterfall with the moon reflecting on it right now is perfect.

I put on my rain boots and walk into the stream, capturing the beauty nature made. I move forward, back to the right and to the left, to get a shot of every angle. I'm so lost in what I'm doing that when I finish, I realize Mandi has been sitting on the log, watching me.

"You can go back to bed," I say, wading through the water to the shore.

"I like watching you work." She hugs her legs. "It's like you see something different through that lens."

"I do. Sometimes when I look back at the pictures, I'm amazed at what I got."

We sit on the log for a moment, neither of us saying anything.

"You've got something special," she finally says.

"Thanks."

"I'm serious, Noah." She places her hand on my thigh. "If you ever stopped photographing the wilderness, the world would be missing out. You give people a peek into a place they'll probably never go and you make it come to life. Don't ever quit."

I turn to her and brush her hair over her shoulder. "And don't ever quit making people feel like they're the most important person in the world."

She laughs and lays her cheek in my palm. "Okay."

"Should we go back to the tent? We have about five hours before the trail is open again."

"And what do you suggest we do with those five hours?"

"Maybe you scream my name, I'll scream yours?"

She laughs and stands, holding out her hand. I accept, and when we're chest to chest, I take her in my arms.

"You know how they say people come into your life for a reason?" I say.

She nods.

"I must have a guardian angel who brought you into my life because you give me purpose. You reinvigorated me just when I thought my time as a freelance photographer for the outdoors might be over."

She rests her chin on my chest and gives me a sad sort of smile. "I'm glad."

"Me too." Even if that truth hurts.

We stand there for a second, our gazes locked. I don't even want to sleep with her for the next five hours. I just want to hold her and imagine a life where she really is mine until death do us part.

But I'm pretty sure her short speech was her goodbye message to me. Her way of telling me it's okay for me to leave after the wedding.

After a minute, she steps back, strips off her shirt, waggles her eyebrows, and disappears into the tent.

And since I'm a man, of course I follow.

Chapter Twenty-one

Mandi

I walk into Noah's makeshift studio in an empty storefront in downtown Sunrise Bay. "I hear there's this hot photographer in town everyone is dying to be photographed by?"

He's setting up a backdrop and turns around and smiles at me.

"Oh, he's got a great ass too."

He finishes whatever he's doing. "Keep that up and I'm going to have to give you a tour of the back room."

"Promise?"

"I have a half hour." He comes up to me and wraps his arms around my waist, kissing the top of my head. "It's weird. Like I have a regular job or something."

"A nine-to-five. What a change that would be, huh?"

"Yeah, although visits from you make it worthwhile."

I hold up my bag of takeout. "Francois made us some tacos."

"I'm surprised he doesn't refer to himself as Felipe when he prepares tacos."

I roll my eyes and he cleans off the table that's serving as the waiting area right now.

Gavin secured the empty building for two weeks so that Noah could do all the city employees' headshots, but also told him he could use it for whatever else for the duration, no questions asked.

"Why does he insist on being called Francois?" Noah asks, accepting the taco from me and unwrapping it.

I shrug. "He feels like Frank sounds like a guy who makes hot dogs on the corner. The guy who screams at you if you don't order fast enough. You'd think he wouldn't care, but he has a bit of a complex because he wasn't officially trained. Sure, he worked under a few people, but when you look at Rome Bailey and his restaurants in the area, he was formally trained and worked under famous chefs in Europe. I'm not sure if he feels in competition with Rome or what."

"Well, Frank makes great food no matter what you call him. He should be happy with that."

We both lift our tacos and cheers. Our moans display what a great chef Francois is. He's never made me one bad dish.

"So, I've been thinking..." I broach the subject I've been nervous to bring up because I'm not sure how he'll take it. "It's time you move out of the inn. You can move in with Chevelle and me. She's rarely there, especially with this new guy she's seeing. And it's only for the next week since the wedding is next weekend."

"God, how did it come so fast?" he asks, and I wish I had an answer.

"I have no clue. When I think of next week at this time, you'll probably be leaving for an excursion." I can't help my frown.

He shakes his head. "I have to finish here, but I was asked to go take pictures at a surf contest in Southern California the week after. I guess one of the usual photographers can't make it."

"Oh, that's nice."

I might be saying the right thing, but knowing he already has his out for after the wedding stings in a way it shouldn't. I walked into this hornet's nest with my eyes wide open—I can't be upset when I get stung.

"Yeah, I'll probably be more into the waves than the surfers themselves." He finishes his taco and tosses the wrapper into the trash can. "It's crazy how many people have stopped by today, asking if I'm opening a studio, because they're interested in pictures of their family."

"Well, we've never had a dedicated family photographer around here. But you'd think in the day of the cell phones, most people would just take their pictures on their phones."

"I have a friend who might be interested in coming here. She does portraits and could make a killing here. Probably just popping up a few times a year would do it." His excitement to pawn this opportunity off on someone else tells me he's not fully enjoying his experience. That small hope that budded inside me that he might fall in love with it wilts and dies.

"Oh, that's nice."

"She does weddings too, which reminds me. I was thinking we should take some pictures of our wedding and have an entire section on your website."

Because that's what I want to look at on my website. My own fake, failed marriage. Men are so stupid sometimes.

"We'll see." I dig into my purse and slide the key over. "This is the key to my place. Chevelle knows you're moving in and she's fine with it."

He nods and finishes his last taco, again throwing the wrapper in the trash. "Great. I'll be over after I finish here. I obviously don't have anything but a suitcase to bring with me, so it won't take me long to pack."

"Well, my room is top of the stairs to the right. If you'd rather sleep in Nikki or Posey's old room, you can."

He scrunches his forehead. "Why would I want to do that?"

I shrug and keep my voice even. "I'm just leaving it up to you."

He stares at me like he usually does when I act out of character. And the truth is, I do feel out of sorts after listening to him speak so casually about leaving, and I feel out of sorts after arriving here. I need to stop though, because we both agreed to what's going to happen.

"I'm sorry, I'm just... it's just the wedding is almost here and I'm a bit stressed."

He takes my hands and pulls me up, leading me to sit on his lap. "I know. I can't believe it, and I still don't have my grandma and dad back on talking terms."

"You'll figure something out. I guess I should go finish things up at the inn so I can be home at the same time you are."

"And I have an appointment coming in soon." He pats my ass for me to stand.

He cleans up our mess and I pick up my purse, heading to the door.

"Okay, so I'll see you at home?" I ask, opening the door.

"Yep."

His smile says nothing is amiss, so why do I feel as though there's something off about us?

I GO for my final dress fitting and my mom joins me since all the last-minute things are done and she's feeling left out.

"How are things?" she says when she gets in my car.

"Perfect. Did you see Gavin gave Noah one of the open storefronts for a studio?" I pull out of her driveway to head to Anchorage.

"I heard about that. Is he going to continue with that after the wedding?" The hesitation in her voice over whether she's overstepping is clear, but it's not like my mom to ever skirt around a topic. She's usually blunt without apology.

"Is that your way of asking if he's going to stay in town?"

"Marriage is hard. Even harder to grow together if he's gone all the time." She stares out the window as if she's not trying to lure me into a conversation.

Pulling onto the highway, I don't say anything right away.

"Have you thought of... traveling with him?" my mom asks.

"No. I don't know." I shrug and swallow hard.

Another round of silence commences. I'm not sure how to take this coming from my mom.

"You should. Travel with him."

I turn to her briefly before putting my attention back on the road. "Why would you say that?"

She shrugs but turns in my direction. "Oh, Mandi. What do you want to do?"

"Um, run the inn. Same as I've been doing all this time."

She frowns for a beat. "Do you though?"

"Okay, Mom, what are you getting at?" I continue to drive, although I wish we weren't having this conversation in the car.

"Don't think I don't appreciate everything you've done for me. All those years after we left Arizona, after Rylan was born. You've always been the one I could depend on. And I've probably taken that for granted. So, I want to ask you what *you* want to do? If it's running the inn, then great. But if it's not, then that's okay too." She pats my knee.

"Can I be honest, Mom?"

She has always been someone we could talk to, but I don't want to insult her either.

"Always."

I draw in a deep breath. "I'm afraid to lose the inn because what if I lose the one thing that gives me a sense of security?" Even if it's not doing well right now, I don't say. "I mean, there's not a career out there I'm dying to do or anything. I love taking care of the inn, taking care of my guests. But even if I hired more employees, traveled with Noah sometimes. Then I lose it all if he ever decides I'm not enough for him."

My mom takes a big breath. "I had a feeling."

"What?"

"That your father's and my divorce scared you. But Noah isn't your dad. Not by a long shot."

"You barely know him," I say, being completely honest, although I've not seen characteristics like my dad's in Noah.

"But I was married to your dad for a long time. I can spot a clone."

I laugh. "I know he's not Dad, but that doesn't mean we won't just fall out of love."

Except we're not even in love. We're in lust if anything.

Seriously, I'm already imagining coming home tonight to find him there and I like it—too much.

"That's the chance you take with love, yes. I took that chance twice, and when it pays off, it pays off big. I've never been happier than with Hank. But I think you already know that. And it was hard with him. He'd been married to a woman he loved very much. His wife died and I always worried I wouldn't compare to Laurie. That's why I promised myself, as hard as it was to be reminded that I was his second wife, there needed to be room in our marriage for her. Especially with her being your stepsiblings' mother."

"You handled it better than most would." I glance at her and smile.

"That doesn't mean it was easy. I might have made it look that way, but it was a struggle. What are you really afraid of with Noah?"

I pull off the highway. "I don't know. He's adventurous, I'm not. He likes to live life to the fullest, see the world, and I enjoy our small town. Maybe we're just different."

"But something drove you together, no?"

I nod. "Yeah, but—"

"Well, you have time. Don't rush anything. You're already rushing getting married. Just let all the other big decisions you have to make soak in more. Maybe after he leaves, that will change your mind or even his. You never know what the future holds, and no one has a crystal ball."

I pull into the parking lot as I mull over her words.

"I can't wait to see how beautiful you look." She opens her door and gets out of the car.

I sit for a second longer, taking in her advice. She's right. I need to relax and let the chips fall where they may.

Brena and Thad greet us as soon as we walk through the bridal shop door.

"We have your dress all ready." Brena beams and walks me to the back.

Thad escorts my mom to the mirrored area with couches.

"I've been excited for you to come in all week." She unzips the bag and there's my dress, fully altered to my dimensions. "You picked a wonderful dress."

I strip down to my corset and underwear, and she opens the dress for me to step in. Once the zipper goes up without a fight, I release a relieved breath and stare at myself in the mirror. I'm so in love with this dress and can't believe I'm wearing this to a fake wedding, for a fake fiancé.

"Let's go show your mom," Brena says.

I walk out of the fitting room, over to the pedestal, and stare at three reflections of me.

My mom comes up behind me, sniffling. "Oh, Mandi."

I smile at her in the mirror, smoothing my hands down the front of my dress. "I know."

I'm actually getting married. Too bad it's not the real thing, because what I feel for Noah is way too real for me to admit to anyone, especially him.

Chapter Twenty-two

Noah

I watch Mandi get out of bed, admiring her naked form before she grabs her robe. I'm not sure what it was, but last night, neither of us could get enough of the other. Just as she was falling asleep, I started to kiss her neck, and when I was drifting, she sneaked under the covers to blow me.

"Do you want in the shower first?" she asks. "And no worries on Chevelle, she leaves super early."

"Go ahead."

She leaves the room and I sit up in bed, wondering how this will all go down. How I'll ever leave Sunrise Bay after we're wed.

Deciding I better just worry about the immediate issues, I unpack my suitcase into the dresser drawers Mandi said I could use, but the first drawer I open has a stack of books in it. I flip through one, instantly realizing these are journals of some sort. One catches my eye as I'm about to move them out of the drawer.

"Dream Wedding." It's in a different handwriting than she uses now, so I assume it was written by a much younger version of herself.

I listen for the shower, knowing this is an intrusion on her privacy, but I want to know what she envisioned for her wedding since she's let everyone else have their way through the planning process. Opening the book, I see cutouts from magazines. Flowers, dresses, bridesmaids' dresses. Whoever Bentley Powers is, I'm annoyed, because she's written her name as Mrs. Bentley Powers or Mrs. Mandi Powers about a hundred times down the page. I'd like to tear out that page and put it through an industrial shredder.

But what I find on the last page is so breathtaking, I wonder if I can replicate it with not a ton of time left.

A couple stands under a wooden arbor with flowers covering most of it. It would be perfect for the outdoor wedding we're planning. Imagine her surprise when she walks out and finds me waiting under one.

The shower stops. A few seconds later, the bathroom door opens, and I hear her say, "Noah, I was thinking. Are people going to think it's weird we're not going on a honeymoon?"

I stuff her wedding book in my camera bag and throw my clothes into the other drawers. "No, we'll just say we're planning one after tourist season is done."

"Oh, that's a good idea." She comes into the room in only her towel.

"Come here," I say, widening my legs.

She does as I ask, and once she's situated between my legs, I untuck the towel and it falls to the floor. "Whoops."

"Really? That's all you got?" She gives me her saucy grin.

I raise my hands and mold them to her tits, my thumbs stroking her nipples. "Well, I could say it one more time before we both have to go to work." I bend down and take one of her nipples in my mouth.

"You really are insatiable."

"And you love it," I say against her damp skin.

"Yeah, I do." She arches her back, offering herself to me.

Next thing I know, I'm on my back and she's above me.

"Shit."

"What?" Her hand slides down my body, gripping my length.

"I'm out of condoms. I was going to go to the store today."

"Well, good thing for you I'm on birth control, but are you clean?" She looks at me like an interrogator, and I laugh.

"I'm clean. It's embarrassing, but I haven't slept with anyone in a long time, and I was tested after. You?"

She nods. "Are you comfortable with it?"

I flip her onto her back. "Is that a trick question?"

I run my hand through her folds to make sure she's ready, and as always, she is. And then I slide the tip of my cock through her folds, focusing on her clit. She groans at the sensation.

"Bet you're wishing you would've told me sooner we could go bare."

"You're delaying it for both of us here." She brings her hands around to grip my ass, trying to pull me forward.

I thrust inside her. "Okay, you're going to play that way, are you?"

Let's just say we're both running late by the time we leave the house. As soon as I crawled out of bed, the countdown timer in my head started up again. Maybe we should have had a longer engagement.

AFTER I TAKE the pictures of all the city employees, I take on Logan, Nikki, and Noah.

"So I want one with Noah kissing my stomach." Nikki lifts her shirt. "Come on, Noah."

Noah ignores his mom because he's too busy giving me a death glare.

"I'm seriously thinking about changing my name and I was Noah first," I say and chuckle.

"You. No. Noah." He slaps his chest. "Me. Noah."

"Okay, buddy." Logan takes his son's hand away from his chest and looks at Nikki. "Is this something we should be talking to someone about? This doesn't seem like normal two-and-a-half-year-old behavior."

"He's fine. He's just pissed that Mandi had to go find a guy named Noah to marry. I mean, there are other men in Alaska."

I clear my throat.

"Not that she didn't find a keeper in you," Nikki is quick to change her tune. "Come on, sweetheart."

Logan looks at Nikki. "You're barely showing."

"We're going to do a progression of them."

Logan looks at me. "Is that something people do? Sounds like something we could do with a cell phone."

"Logan!" Nikki scolds.

Baby Noah walks across the room and stomps on my foot. Good to constantly know where I stand with this kid.

"I don't do a lot of portraits, so I wouldn't know what's in right now," I tell Logan.

"Well, it is in. You can trust me." Nikki waves as though our opinions are of little concern.

Logan blows out a breath. "I guess we'll be seeing each other every month."

He stands beside his wife in their color-coordinated outfits. I snap a few pictures, and we do one of just Nikki and Noah. I get him to not fixate on me long enough to take a cute picture of him kissing his mom's belly.

By the time we're done, it feels as if we just started.

"Thanks, Noah. Let me know what I owe you." Nikki says.

"Yeah, right." Taking money from Mandi's family feels weird. I'm used to doing pictures for people I know as favors.

"Thanks again." She smiles and they walk out, Noah turning around and staring me down the entire time.

Next, Posey comes in with baby Shay nestled into her carrier. "Gavin's going to meet us here. Thank you so much for doing this."

"It's not a problem." I snap a picture of Shay in her carrier. "I'm going to be honest, I've never done newborn photography or even moved one around."

"It's okay, I did a YouTube tutorial today. We're going to wrap her up like a burrito, and I had a bed delivered to Gavin, which he's bringing."

"A bed?"

"A dog bed." Posey pulls Shay out of the carrier, and she coos. "And no worries, she should sleep through the entire thing."

"I hope so." I'm a little nervous the kid will wake up and start screaming.

Gavin comes in a few minutes later with a big box in his hands. "Seriously, Posey, you couldn't order it to the house?"

"I wasn't going to be able to carry it with her. What do you think I am, an octopus?"

Gavin smiles at me. "Hey, Noah. Thanks for this."

"No problem. Let's get started."

Posey looks at Gavin. "Where are the clothes?"

"Shit. Start with Shay and I'll be back." He leaves again.

Posey cringes. "Sorry, we're not usually like this, but we're running on minimal sleep."

"No apologies. I have no idea what it would be like to have a kid."

"Not yet anyway." She smiles as though kids are on the horizon for me. Little does she know.

Posey positions Shay like a pro, and if this was my usual gig, I think I'd hire her as an assistant. We get some cute pictures of Shay in different poses, and when Gavin returns, we do some family poses, then a few of just Posey and Gavin.

When we're done, Posey writes down her phone number and tells me to text her the total and that she'll transfer it over to me. I hate taking the money since I really don't need it, but in preparation for today I did some digging on the going rate and realized I forgot how well portraits pay.

At lunch, I walk down to the diner, and on the way, Amy from Twisted Stem stops me. "Hey, Noah, I heard you opened a studio?"

"It's only temporary, but I did agree to take a few pictures for some people. Do you need something?"

"I just wondered if you could come by and take a few pictures. I'm thinking about making some brochures, and I want to increase my online presence like you did for Mandi."

I forgot how fast news goes around in a small town. "I have some time tomorrow. I'll swing by."

"That would be great. And congratulations on the upcoming nuptials. Mandi is the best, and the fact you two have found one another... well, it's awesome."

I smile at her. "Thank you."

Before I reach the diner, I also get stopped by Theo at

the pottery place. Lastly, Tad from Two Brothers and an Egg asks me to take pictures of their food for their menu.

I should've figured that what's known as different kinds of photography in big cities all fall under the same umbrella here. Knowing I only have less than two weeks before I leave, I hate to leave anyone hanging. I tell everyone yes, though I don't know how I'm going to get them all done.

By the time the day is over and I'm alone in my studio, I'm looking through the pictures I took, ready to edit them on the computer, and I realize I enjoyed the day. Seeing all the happy families and the interactions between them. Even when I had a hard time reining Noah in, it was kind of fun.

The door opens. I expect it to be Mandi, but I'm surprised to see Hank.

"Hey, Hank." I get up from my computer.

We shake hands. Now that I think about it, he's kind of someone I wanted to talk to.

"This space is nice." He looks around. "A lot you could do here." Spoken like a true contractor. "I wanted to see if you needed any help getting it ready. We could probably divide it into two studios." He continues to walk around the place, assessing.

"Oh, I'm not sure. Gavin only contracted me to have it for two weeks."

Hank turns around and faces me. "So where will you shoot when you're in town?"

I shrug. "I'm not sure I will."

He nods, but it's clear he doesn't agree with me spending the majority of our marriage away from Mandi and I can't say I blame him.

"I have a question for you, Hank."

"Sure." He sits at the table and fiddles with my appointments handwritten on a piece of paper.

"There's this arbor." I pull Mandi's wedding book out of my camera bag. "Had I found it earlier, I would've asked, but I just found it. Mandi has been so complacent with planning the wedding, not wanting to inconvenience anyone and letting everyone else have what they want. I'm willing to help, just let me know what I can do. But I was wondering... can we get this done before the wedding? As a surprise for Mandi?"

He looks it over and smiles. "Yeah. It was what I came here to discuss with you. When Mandi was younger, the girls would always talk about their weddings and their grooms. None of them have gone how they used to say they would, but Mandi's number one was always that her groom would be waiting under an arbor covered in flowers. So, when she announced the wedding, I started on one. Having this picture at least tells me the color and some of the details she wants. I came here to let you know, since I wanted it to be a surprise for her."

"You already started it? If you couldn't do it, I was gonna try to find one."

"No need. I have to say, I wasn't really sold on the idea of you two. Such a fast wedding and you hadn't even been introduced to the family. Not really Mandi's style. But this." He pushes his finger down on the picture of the arbor. "Gives me a good feeling about the two of you." He stands and clamps me on the shoulder. "Have a nice night, Noah."

He leaves the makeshift studio and I'm left wondering how many other people are questioning whether our marriage is on the up-and-up.

Chapter Twenty-three

Mandi

It's two days before the wedding and my nerves are on edge. Rather than bachelor and bachelorette parties, we opted to do low-key male/female get-togethers.

All the girls and I had a nice dinner at Dori's grandson's restaurant, Terra and Mare, in Lake Starlight, and the guys just drank beers at Truth or Dare Brewery. Nothing exciting, but Noah's mom and Midge did sit beside each other at dinner and spent the entire night talking, which gave me hope that his dad's attitude toward his mom might soften sometime soon.

So, Noah and I have tonight together, then we've agreed to stay apart the night before the wedding. Actually, my mom demanded that we don't spend the night before the wedding together.

I'm at the inn when a courier service walks in.

"Hi," I greet him.

"I have a delivery for Amanda Greene." He holds out an envelope.

"That's me." I accept the envelope, but there's nothing written on the outside except my name. I tip the guy and he leaves.

Sitting in the chair behind reception, I open the envelope, wondering if it's something for the wedding.

Inside is an invitation for a one-night stay at Glacier Point Resort that's to be used tonight. Dinner in the room, massages for two, and it's made out to Mr. and Mrs. Noah Winters.

Trina walks in a second later with her overnight bag in hand.

"I'm on tonight," I tell her.

"Nope. I was given clear instructions that you are to be off tonight. An early honeymoon or something?" She puts her bag behind the desk.

"But—"

She grabs my purse from under the desk and shoves it into my chest. "You go."

"Okay." I leave, not understanding who this came from, but call Noah on the way back home.

"I don't understand," he says.

"Neither do I, but we have a reservation at Glacier Point tonight in Lake Starlight. Meet me at home?"

God, that sounds so weird.

"I'm just finishing up and I'll meet you there."

We hang up, and I drive the rest of the way home. After thinking about it for a bit, I decide I know who this early wedding present is from. The only thing I don't understand is why they'd demand we go to the resort tonight.

When I arrive home, I walk in, and the family room is dark. I flick on the lights and two bodies scramble on the couch. I'm standing behind the couch, but I can see that it's Chevelle and who I guess is her new boyfriend. She's yet to introduce him to anyone in the family but is bringing him to my wedding.

"Oh, I'm so sorry."

Chevelle quickly gets off the couch and stands to face me. "Hey, Mandi. Um... this is Derek."

The guy doesn't stand, just looks over his shoulder and gives me a wave.

"Hi, Derek." I look back at Chevelle. "So, Noah is on his way home and we're going to Glacier Point for the night. Someone gave us a gift certificate, but we have to use it tonight."

Chevelle rolls her eyes. "You know who it's from, right?"

I nod. "The grandmas. I figure Dori's grandson-in-law owns the resort, so they probably swindled some deal or annoyed him until he finally gave in. You know what they're like."

"I hope one day I'm in the position to get all these luxury things."

I raise an eyebrow. "Luxury things? Chevelle, need I remind you of your bridesmaid's dress?"

"Babe, I thought we were watching a movie," Derek says from the couch.

"In a minute." She holds up her finger.

He blows out an annoyed breath. I glance at him but only see the back of his head.

"You know they're doing this because they think it will seal the deal," Chevelle says.

My forehead wrinkles. "Seal the deal?"

"I know, right? If only they were in the room next door to you guys every night, they'd know how real this is."

I drop my bag. "You mean they don't think Noah and I are really together?" Panic has my heart fluttering.

She shrugs. "Just Dori and Ethel. They kept grilling me at dinner the other night, but I didn't think you'd want me telling Grandma that your screaming could wake a family of hibernating bears."

My cheeks grow hot. "Thank you for that."

The door opens and Noah spots the back of Derek's head where he sits on the couch. "Who are you?"

Hearing the deep voice, Derek shifts on the couch to look behind him. "Who are you?"

Noah stares at Derek as if he's sizing him up.

"That's Derek." I motion between him and Chevelle, and Noah nods at him.

"So, let me see this gift certificate," Noah says. I pull it from my bag and he inspects it. "You can thank whoever this is for your good night's sleep tonight." He winks at Chevelle.

The three of us laugh.

"Chevelle—movie?" Derek says in a stern voice.

Noah looks at me. I try not to make a big deal of the fact that Chevelle's new boyfriend seems like kind of a douche. That's a conversation between stepsisters for another time.

"I said a minute," she says.

Noah leaves my side and sits on the chair adjacent to the couch. "So, you're seeing Chevelle, huh?"

Derek barely glances in his direction. "Yeah."

"Are you from Sunrise Bay?"

"No, I'm just passing through."

Noah's eyes narrow. "I'm sorry?"

"I'm working on one of the fishing boats."

Noah nods. Chevelle is smiling from ear to ear. I have no idea what she sees in this guy.

"Cool. Well, I guess I'll see you at the wedding." Noah gets up off the chair.

"Oh, you're the poor son of a bitch getting hitched, huh?" Derek laughs.

Okay, now I really want to pull Chevelle into the other room and ask her why on earth she's with this guy.

Derek laughs some more. "Totally joking. Congrats, man, that's awesome." His personality flips, and I have no idea if it's because Noah is now towering over him or what, but Noah looks at me.

"Let's go, Mandi."

We go upstairs and pack our bags, leaving Chevelle to entertain Derek The Douche.

"This place is so much nicer than the inn," I whisper to Noah when a bellhop takes our bags.

"You serve very different clientele. Remember that." Noah leads the way to the reception area.

The woman who helps us is overly friendly, especially after seeing our gift certificate. When Noah tries to hand over his credit card, she says all incidentals are taken care of already and to enjoy our night in their luxury suite.

We follow the directions to the elevator and take it to the top floor.

"I feel like I'm supposed to carry you over the threshold, but we're not married yet." He scans the key card and the green light shines for us to open the door.

I step in and stop, Noah walking right into my back. "Holy crap," I say.

He walks around me. "It's nice, but I like the inn more."

"Oh, come on." I slip off my shoes and run to the plush bed, falling onto the king-size mattress. "This is magical."

He falls down right next to me, and I bounce in the air before the mattress settles. "It's okay. I like the homey feel of the inn though."

I straddle him, my hands splayed on his chest. "Stop it. You know this is nice."

"I didn't say it wasn't nice. I said I like the inn more."

I bend down and kiss him once. "You're sweet."

"I can be sweeter." His hand inches up the hem of my blouse. "It's been a long day without you."

"You've been a busy bee over at the makeshift studio." I climb off him and look at the room service menu. "How's it going?"

He sits up and takes my feet in his hands, massaging them. It's a habit of his I've come to love. "I forgot how fun it is to do portraits. Usually, it's just me and an unknowing subject, but I enjoy the interaction with other people and how satisfying it is when you get a kid to smile at the camera. I told one kid today that I was Thor, and the parents were thrilled. But everyone is so happy. I forgot there were families out there like that."

I wiggle my toes. "Yeah. Anything new with your dad and grandma?"

"Nothing yet. So, how much do I have to pay you to have a kid?"

I laugh, and thankfully, so does he. We're already walking a thin line.

"Hopefully, my mom will do some convincing."

"Maybe we can get them to dance together at the wedding," I say, and he nods.

"We'll have some opportunities after we're married when I'm not traveling. I really thought before the wedding would be our best shot, but my father is so damn stubborn."

A big part of me wants to suggest that he stick around town so he can be sure they repair their relationship, but that's not what we agreed on. It wouldn't be fair for me to change the plan now.

"Why am I giving you a foot massage when we have one booked downstairs?"

I chuckle. "Very true. What did she say?" I ask, since the receptionist told him what time we need to be down at the spa.

"Seven o'clock. Want to eat after?"

"Yes, but." I glance at the clock. "That still leaves us an hour." I crawl to him. "What should we do with that hour, do you think?"

"We could do the table assignments," he offers.

I touch his forehead with my wrist. "Are you feeling okay? Who wants to do table assignments?"

"Did you have something else in mind?" He smirks as though he likes playing this game.

"I do... and I think you're really going to enjoy it." I get down on my knees on the richly carpeted floor and unbutton his jeans.

His hand lands on mine so I can't slide down the zipper. "Nah, I need to be inside you."

He stands and pulls me up by my hand, wrapping his arm around me and lowering me to the bed. He stares at me for longer than I'm comfortable with, and I squirm.

"Now that you have me in the bed, what will you do with me?"

"I'd like to kidnap you, so I never have to live a day without you." He flicks open the button of my pants. Then he unzips them, and I lift my ass so he can tug them down my legs and dispose of them on the floor. "I love these panties."

He trails his knuckle along the wetness of my panties like he always does. Like someone dipping their toe into the pool before they plunge. I open my legs for him, and he slides the thin fabric over, exposing my pussy to the cool, air-conditioned room. His finger brushes along my clit, and our eyes lock, his filled with a hunger I'll never get tired of.

"I love fucking you," he says.

For a moment there, I thought he said I fucking love you and I just about stopped breathing.

I bite my lip and he undoes his pants, allowing them to pool at his feet.

"I want your ass up in the air." He takes my hips and flips me around so I'm on my stomach. His fingers hook in both sides of my panties, and he drags them down, leaving them at my knees. "Spread those legs, beautiful."

I do as he says.

He climbs up on the bed and runs his cock through my folds, wetting the tip before pushing into me.

"Noah," I pant.

His one hand lands on the small of my back and he thrusts inside me. "Always so wet for me. Tell me I'm the only man who makes you this drenched."

"Only you," I say.

And in that fancy hotel room, Noah fucks me like he never has before. As if he owns me. I can't deny that a large part of me will stay with Noah after he leaves, because I'll never be able to forget these moments when he made me feel so sexy and desirable.

When we're finished and he comes inside me, we both crash on the bed for a moment before he cleans me up with a washcloth from the bathroom.

"I really don't want to leave this room," he says, getting dressed.

"Me either, but for a massage, I think it might be worth it." I begin to dress too.

"You want someone else's hands on you other than mine?" He kisses me briefly while retrieving his shirt.

"Never, I'd pick your hands over anyone else's."

He winks. "Good girl."

I allow my words to soak in because pretty soon, no one's hands will be on me because he'll be in Southern California with a bunch of surfers.

Chapter Twenty-four

Mandi

"I'll admit, I've never had a massage before, but that will not be my last," Noah says on the way back up to our hotel room.

"I agree. I'm not usually up for other people touching me, but I feel like Calgon took me away."

Noah laughs. "What?"

"You've never heard that expression before?"

He swipes the key card to unlock the door to our room. "No."

"My mom used to say it all the time. It was some old-time slogan from a bubble bath or something."

"I feel like they don't make the slogans like they used to." He pushes the door open for me to enter first.

"Definitely not." I lie down on the bed and sigh in relaxed bliss.

Noah picks up the room service menu. "And now we eat."

I sit up and rest my chin on his shoulder, peering over to see what I want to order. Sometimes I'm amazed how comfortable I am with Noah after only a couple months, but I guess we threw ourselves into this mess. Something about us being on the same side, on the same team, has brought us together.

He opts for a steak, and I order chicken. We pick two different potato options to share. Once Noah has called it in, I turn on the television.

"Should we binge-watch something?" I sign into my Netflix account.

He tugs at the belt of my robe. "I have something better in mind."

I swat his hand. "The food is going to be here soon."

"The food's not going to be here for a while." He makes quick work of the belt and his hands mold to my hips and brings me down on the mattress.

"I have no idea what you're going to do without me when you leave. You seem to not be able to go a few hours without having sex."

His hands slide between the terrycloth robe and my skin, and he hovers over me. "Believe me, I've thought about it every fucking day. It's like I can't breathe without you in the room." His mouth descends on my neck, and he sprinkles little kisses on my skin.

My breathing grows shallow. I'm glad I'm not the only one who feels that way.

I let him distract me from both of us having to come to reality and realize our little rendezvous is almost over.

His thigh spreads my legs apart and he situates himself between my legs.

I push his robe off his large shoulders, and he takes a moment to get his arms out and toss it away. He bends down and covers my nipple with his mouth, sucking and swirling my nipple with his tongue, while his other hand squeezes my other breast. The tip of his cock teases my opening.

"God, tell me this isn't our last time together," he murmurs.

I have no idea how to answer him, because it very well

could be. So I decide to go with a hopeful answer. "We have all night."

He raises his head and locks eyes with me. "You know what I mean. I want to take my time with you, make sure I've memorized and savored every inch of your body so I can relive it on those cold nights up north. When I know I'll be wishing you were with me."

I cling to him tighter, and his mouth covers mine, searing me with a kiss I'm certain to never forget.

His tongue slides against mine in a dance that we've perfected over the weeks, and he slides into me, unhurried. Maybe because we both know our time is coming to an end, but this time, we're not fucking. The end goal is not an orgasm, but to savor each moment with each other, fearful of what happens when it's over. Like cherishing your final few bites of the best dessert you've ever tasted.

His one hand grips my breast as he slides unhurriedly in and out of me, over and over. His tongue and mouth tease me with kisses, and he purposely hits every place he's found over the weeks that drive me crazy. I grab his ass and squeeze as he continues to grind and thrust in and out of me.

Emotion swells in my chest until I think I might burst. "Oh, Noah."

"I know," he whispers.

There's so much truth in those four words. As if we're on the same page but can't bear to say what we're feeling.

I savor every touch, every second, and when my orgasm crests and my body pleads for release, I hold back for as long as I can, because what if I never experience something like this again?

"God, Mandi."

I look up to see a pained expression on his face. One that suggests he's doing the same as me.

"Please," I say, and he thrusts inside me deeper. I wrap my legs around his waist.

Then he's on top of me, his mouth at my ear, his breath labored, his words loving. He doesn't tell me what he's going to do to me next, but he says how good I feel, how nobody has ever had this effect on him. I confess how he makes me feel, and my orgasm climbs to a level I cannot control.

"I'm going to come," I say, almost breathless.

He picks up his head, his gaze steady with mine while he watches me unravel. My body free-falls into bliss. "I'll never get the way you look when you come out of my head."

His lips crash to mine and he thrusts into me over and over, our hands frantic and searching as though we're both trying to grab something we can hold on to and keep for ourselves after this is over. He tenses inside me, and I feel the warmth of his release pour into me.

Noah lies on me, not giving me his full weight, and his hand brushes the sweat-soaked hair from my forehead while he kisses me long and languid. I never want to leave this bed—or him.

I could be wrong, but I'm pretty sure Noah and I complicated our relationship even more because we just made love.

FOR THE REST of the night, we eat dinner, watch reruns of *Friends,* and eventually make it into the bathtub.

"They have flower petals!" I pick them up and sprinkle them in the hot water.

"And candles." He lights a match from the book they supply and lights the candles.

Once we're standing in the flicker of candlelight, Noah brushes my robe off over my shoulders and it pools to the floor.

"Ladies first." He takes my hand as I step into the oversized tub and sink into the hot water.

A minute later, he joins me. Even after seeing him naked for weeks, his body still puts me in a state of awe. He's so big, so masculine, and makes me feel feminine and small.

He takes my foot in his hands as we sit facing one another. "You feel far away."

"Pretty soon I'll be thousands of miles away." There's a layer of regret in my voice.

The smile drops from his face. "Can we not talk about it for tonight? I just want to enjoy this time with you and not think of what's to come."

I nod. "Okay."

He stares at my foot while his thumbs dig into it. "I don't have a foot fetish, but I do love your feet. I like the way your nails are always painted some shade of pink."

"Pink is girly." I wiggle my toes.

He meets my gaze. "Truth?"

I bite my lip for a second, then nod. "Yeah."

"I've never had anything like this with someone before. I've never had a long relationship. Maybe because I was always traveling, but I like how well we've gotten to know each other."

"Same. I mean, I've dated different guys for a few months at a time, but usually the dates were sporadic and not all condensed like this. I never got to know any of them as well as I know you. I like having someone on my side."

He nods. "I think that's it. I've lived such a solitary life for so long, and now here you are, and you listen to my problems, try to guide me, help me, support me, and I love that."

"Do you think that's natural, or do you think it happened because of the arrangement we made? We've had to keep a secret together from everyone we love."

He's quiet for a moment, probably pondering my question. "Even before the arrangement, I felt it with you. There's just something about you that I'm drawn to, Mandi."

I smile, running my thumb across a flower petal. "I hope I don't end up an old maid. Like the aunt who rarely dates and is always available to watch her nieces and nephews." I frown at the thought.

"That could never happen. You're way too amazing of a person for some guy not to come and knock you off your feet."

I want to tell him that he did that and I'm pretty sure he's fallen for me like I have him, but here he is, ready to throw me back in the pond. But I don't want to make him feel bad. I knew the score going in.

"Maybe we make a new deal," he says with a smirk.

"What's that?"

"After I'm too old to travel and if neither of us finds someone, we marry for real."

I laugh. "Well, to be honest, I hope it doesn't come to that, but just in case, I'll take the deal."

He huffs. "It'll probably be me coming back and finding you happy with a doting husband and kids. I'll be the bastard who didn't know how good he had it."

"Don't say things like that," I say, mostly because it hurts that he's still so certain about leaving. I'm on the fence, practically ready to jump on the next plane with him, but he hasn't even considered changing his life for me.

"It's the truth. In every movie, it's the guy like me who

ends up alone, regretting his decisions and those forks in the road he didn't take."

I wiggle my other foot. "I thought we weren't going to talk about this tonight?"

"True. I don't want to sulk on one of my last nights with you."

We change the subject, talking about high school and laughing about our first kisses. He tells me the story of when he first slept with a girl and how awkward it was that her dog stared at him the entire time, and I laugh a lot.

After we're prunes, we slide into bed naked and hold each other, continuing to enjoy one another's company until our eyelids are too heavy and we fall asleep.

Hands down, the best night of my life.

And possibly the worst—because I know it will never happen with this man again.

Noah

$\mathscr{I}$ walk into Northern Lights Retirement Center to talk with Grandma about mending her relationship with my dad. If I'm going to all this trouble to marry Mandi and we're deceiving her entire family, I need them to heal what's broken between them.

Dori and Ethel are walking down the hall as I enter the building. They stop, look at one another, and back at me. God, they're so manipulative.

"Heard you and Mandi had a surprise gift last night?" Ethel says.

"Like the two of you didn't set it up." I shake my head. "Thank you. It was a very relaxing night right before the chaos of the wedding." I hug and kiss each one on the cheek.

"Who said it was us?" Dori looks at Ethel, then they continue their way down the hall.

"Knock, sweetie, you never know who your grandma has over," Ethel calls.

A shiver runs through my body as I turn toward my grandma's apartment. I knock and she answers, fully dressed. Thank God.

"Oh, Noah." Her words are stilted, as if maybe someone is here on a conjugal visit.

I glance over her shoulder. "Do you have company?"

She opens the door. "No, I just wasn't expecting you."

I step in and see her checkbook out on the table with a bunch of envelopes. "Paying bills?"

She shuffles over to the table before I can and uses both her arms to pile it all together, obviously making sure I don't see a thing.

"What's with the secrets?" I eye her while she shoves a knitted placemat over all the papers.

"Nothing. Just... what brings you by? Want something to drink? We could go out."

I cross my arms. "Grandma?"

She pushes up her dark glasses. "What?"

"I'm not an idiot, what are you hiding from me?" I walk over to the table.

She places herself between the table and me, but she doesn't block my view since I'm at least a foot taller than her. I glance over at the pile but can't really see much.

"It's just a wedding present for you and Mandi." She smiles and pats me on the chest.

"You don't have to give us anything."

"Nonsense. You need a nest egg to start." She steps to the side, assuming I'm done snooping, but I pick up a piece of paper peeking out from under the placemat.

"Nest egg?"

The paper has a list of accounts with an ungodly amount of money in each. I knew she had to have made money when she sold the company, but not this much. And I had figured living in Northern Lights would have taken a huge chunk of that money.

"What's this?" I hold up the paper.

She snatches it from my grip. "Stop being so nosy."

"Answer the question. How do you have all this money?"

She shrugs. "I sold the company. You know this. I'm smart and invested the money."

"You have all these different accounts? Why is it divided up like that?"

She sits down on her sofa. "Tomorrow, after you marry Mandi, you'll be receiving your money."

My forehead wrinkles. "My money?"

"The account I opened for you after I sold the company, if you must know. I wanted it to be a surprise."

"Well, I'm surprised now. Shocked is probably a better word." I sit on the couch with her. "What about Mom and Dad?"

She exhales as if I'm pulling a magician's secrets out of her. "They're getting theirs too." She waves it off as if it's not a big deal.

"Why did you hold out on giving them theirs?" I understand a little better why my dad would be mad. I guess I was too young to realize what she would have made off the sale. My parents struggled until my dad was able to make a name for himself in the art world and open up a studio in Anchorage.

"That's between me and your dad." She folds the paper. "Are you happy, Noah?"

Her quick change of subject gives me whiplash. "What? Yeah."

"I mean being a photographer. Is it a profession you love? Do you wake up every morning happy you get to do it?"

"Why are you asking?" I lean back on the couch.

"I just want to make sure you're happy." She pats my knee.

I shake my head, not understanding exactly what she's looking for. Some sort of confirmation?

"You don't have to give that money to Mandi and me. Save it for yourself." Jesus, if I thought I felt guilty about lying about this whole thing before, it's going to triple if my grandma insists on giving me this money.

She shakes her head. "It's my wedding present to you. I'm sorry I didn't give it to you earlier, but I have my reasons."

Which I don't ask about because it doesn't really matter at this point.

"It's too much, Grandma."

"You guys are free to do with it what you want."

I blow out a breath and lower my head, staring at the floor, guilt consuming me.

"Noah, is there something you want to tell me?"

For a moment, I consider telling her all of it. That the marriage is a farce and I roped an innocent girl into marrying me in an as-yet-failed attempt to end this family feud.

"I have to go." I stand and bend down to kiss her cheek. "I'll see you at the wedding tomorrow."

"Noah," she calls, but I walk out of her apartment, down the hall, and out the doors of the retirement center.

I'm not mad at my grandma. In fact, I'm prepared to give Mandi the entire check to get the inn back on its feet. I just don't understand why my grandma would keep the money from my father when giving it to him might have fixed their relationship.

I DECIDE NOT to drive over to Mandi's because she has last-minute wedding stuff to handle, so I head to Hank and Marla's. I have no idea how he's hiding the arbor from

Mandi, but when I pull up in the driveway, I see a big work tent set up on the driveway.

Marla comes out of the house with a tray. "Noah?" She smiles at me. "I was just bringing Hank some lunch. Do you want something?"

I shake my head. "No, thank you. I figured I'd stop by and check on the surprise."

She tilts her head. "You and Hank are keeping this very tight lipped. He won't even let me see it." She hands me the tray. "I was going to sneak a peek, but go ahead and bring him his lunch. Tell him he has to eat it all, including the smoothie." She shakes her head. "You'd think a cancer survivor would take better care of himself."

I walk into the tent and find Hank hand carving some of the wood around the top of the arbor. I hold up the tray.

He shakes his head. "I heard her."

"Then you heard you have to finish the green smoothie?"

"She tracks everything I eat since I was diagnosed. But what are you gonna do? I know she does it out of love. Scared the crap out of her and it would've me if our roles were reversed. That's love for you." He shrugs.

I stand back and admire the arbor. "Hank, I'm speechless. It's beautiful."

"Thanks. Amy is going to come over and put up the flowers first thing tomorrow morning. They'll match all the other ones you guys picked out. Then I'm driving it over to the inn while the girls have her locked in a room, getting ready. I recruited her brothers to help me. I know you'll be busy." He wipes his hands on a rag, then comes to stand next to me and looks at the arbor. "I forgot how much I love working on special projects like this. I can't wait to see her face."

Just the thought of her surprised face brings a smile to my face. "Me either."

"I'm probably not telling you anything new here, but Mandi is such a giver to everyone else, she deserves someone who will give her the world. Someone who'll give her everything she needs, which isn't much. All she really needs from someone is love and commitment." He picks up his sandwich and takes a bite.

"She's definitely someone special."

He glances at me, but I don't know what else to say. At some point after we've divorced, Hank will recall this conversation and feel as if I bullshitted my way through it when in fact, I agree with everything Hank said. I desperately wish I was that man. He'll never know how much I prayed I was.

"Thanks a lot."

Hank shakes his head. "I know you had the idea like I did, but I'm doing this for Mandi."

"Of course." I nod, shake his hand, and leave the tent, heading back to my truck.

I drive over to Mandi and Chevelle's apartment and spot Mandi's car there, so when I walk in and hear sex noises, I freeze. Listening, I quickly realize they're coming from upstairs. What the fuck? I tiptoe up the stairs, my stomach bottoming out at the sound of moaning and the slapping of flesh coming from Mandi's room.

I get to Mandi's door and turn the knob, opening it to find Mandi spread eagle on her bed with a vibrator between her legs and a porno playing on her TV.

She quickly gets up, her face tomato red. "Noah!"

"I wasn't enough to satisfy you last night?" I watch the porno until Mandi clicks it off.

"The opposite. I don't want to climb you all the time and

I thought we weren't seeing one another today. I just had to take the edge off."

I walk over to the bed and pick up the vibrator, turning it on. "Lie down, Mandi."

"No way, I'm embarrassed enough." She's covering her face with her hands.

"Lie down."

She does what I ask the second time, and I trail the vibrator up her inner thigh, wiggling it a bit to entice her to spread her legs.

"Open for me." She does and I keep it at the lowest speed, purposely staying away from her clit. "Turn on the porno now."

"God, Noah!"

"Come on. I'm going to be your husband. We have no secrets."

She bites her lip and grabs the remote, turning the porno back on. I use the vibrator on her, getting her so close but taking away the pleasure before she climaxes. I'm hard as a rock by the time I let her come. She cries out and tries to close her legs, but I force her to keep them open.

Once she comes down from her orgasm, I watch her eyes flutter open and a sweet, soft smile creases her lips. "Thank you?"

I chuckle. "You're welcome."

"Now your turn." She reaches for my jeans, but I still her with my hands over hers.

"I'm good. I love watching you get off."

"And I love watching you." Her lids are still heavy.

I shake my head. "I have some news for you."

She stiffens for a moment. "You look serious. I'd like to put some pants on." She climbs off the bed.

"Well that's a shame."

She smiles at me over her shoulder, and I wish I had my camera to snap this picture.

Once she's dressed, she sits on the bed beside me. "What is it?"

I press my lips into a thin line. "It turns out my grandma is going to give us a large sum of money tomorrow after the wedding. She's referring to it as a nest egg. I'm going to give it to you as a thank you and for you to invest in the inn."

"Noah, no." She shakes her head adamantly. "That's your family money."

"I want to, and I figured you'd be excited. At least you get something out of this."

Her expression turns soft, and she takes my hand. "I got a lot out of this. And business will pick up eventually. We've made some great improvements. I'm not worried."

I look deeply into her eyes. God, I cannot imagine being even a five-minute drive from her—how the hell am I going to handle being hours and hours away?

"Please let me do this for you. As a thank you for giving up so much for me." I tuck a piece of her fiery hair behind her ear.

"Noah, I—"

"What?"

She hesitates, then shakes her head. "Nothing. You better go before my sisters get here. They're planning a whole night of bachelorette fun."

"I thought we said no bachelorette?"

"It's just them sleeping over honestly. Probably baked me a penis cake or something." She rolls her eyes good-naturedly.

"I can't remember what it's even like to sleep without you." I kiss her forehead.

"I know. I guess we have to get used to it though, right?"

Neither of us smiles. I wish I knew what she was going to say a moment ago, but at this point, what does it matter?

The doorbell rings downstairs, and I take her head in my hands, drawing her lips to mine. I kiss her with everything I feel in this moment. How scared I am for this to end. How much I've enjoyed our time together. How I can't think of a better person in the world than her. And when I close the kiss, her cheeks are pink and she's heaving for a breath.

"I'll see you tomorrow." I kiss her one last time and she leans in, hugging me.

"Tomorrow," she mumbles before inhaling deeply.

"What is this?" Nikki screeches from the doorway. "Nope. No way. You have her for the rest of your life, we get her tonight."

We break apart and our gazes remain on one another until Nikki pulls me out of the bedroom.

"Bye-bye, Noah." Nikki waves and slams the door in my face.

How can I already miss her? And what the hell am I going to do when it's time for me to leave Alaska?

Chapter Twenty-six

Mandi

All my sisters are still asleep when I pour coffee into a to-go mug and head out to the bay. I need to clear my head before I start getting ready.

Ever since Noah told me about the money last night, I can't stop thinking that we're making a mistake. He should want me to sign a prenup or something. I'd never take a dime of that money, let alone all of it like Noah wants.

He's been so kind and caring these past few weeks. Actually, the entire time I've known him. If I'm completely honest, I've fallen in love with him. That realization should bring me happiness. Instead, I just feel misery.

I sip my coffee and walk the path along the bay, passing some tourists and people from town. I didn't think this would be so hard, but this pit in my stomach just won't go away.

Since I promised Noah I'd marry him, I'm going to follow through. It feels as though I'm willingly signing myself up for heartbreak, but I probably should've known that was the case before.

My phone vibrates in my pocket, and when I pull it out, I see a text from Noah.

I miss you.

There's a picture of the empty spot next to him in bed.

I smile at the phone and walk up the pathway back to my place.

You'd think I had been gone for hours the way the house is in a frenzy when I return.

"There you are! Where have you been? I was just about to call you." Chevelle pulls me by my arm into my bedroom. "Posey needs to do everyone's hair and makeup."

I sit for Posey, and she curls my hair into long ringlets and does my makeup with a natural look like I requested. I couldn't be happier that my sister is the one doing my bridal look. Since I decided to slide into my dress at the inn, I sit back and stare out the window while the rest of my sisters get ready. Posey is the last one finished since she has to do her own hair and makeup.

"I can't believe you're getting married," Posey says while she puts on mascara.

"Me either," I confess.

"And Chevelle, who is this Derek guy? Could you be next?" Nikki's eyebrows rise.

Chevelle finishes her lip gloss and shrugs. "I don't know. He can be kind of a dick. We got into it the other night. He apologized after and said he's just stressed from work, but it didn't sit well with me. He'll be at the wedding though, so you can all meet him."

I keep my mouth shut since I don't really care for him.

"The bride is way too quiet." Nikki looks at me. "What's up?"

"Nothing. Just nervous about saying my vows in front of everyone." What am I going to say? I'm marrying a man who doesn't love me? A man who I'm in love with, but that only makes things harder? I'm so confused.

I take a deep breath and try to settle my stomach.

"That's why you should've just run away," Posey says. "I'm thinking about a courthouse wedding now."

"Really?" Chevelle asks.

She shrugs. "We already have a kid. And I don't know... Gavin wants it, like, now. Says he's the mayor and blah, blah, blah."

We all laugh.

"All I know is you should do what you want," Nikki says, and all three of them look at me.

"What?" I ask.

They all shrug.

"You wanted a small wedding and Mom got you to agree to make it bigger," Posey says.

"Oh whatever, you practically murdered Gavin just so Mom could win the mayoral race and be happy. We all want Mom to be happy."

Nikki sits down closer to me. "You're happy, right? With Noah?"

My forehead wrinkles. "Yes, why would you ask that?"

She shrugs. "Just making sure. You tend to deal with your problems by yourself and never share much with us."

"That's not true." My lips press into a thin line.

"Come on, Mandi, ever since Mom and Dad divorced, you've put your own needs and wants to the side. I just want to make sure Noah is what you want," she says.

The funny thing is Noah *is* what I want, but I don't like the way I'm getting him.

"Girls!" my mom shouts. "Your ride is here."

Nikki waits while Posey and Chevelle collect their things to take to the inn. "He is what I want, Nik. I wouldn't marry him if he wasn't."

She embraces me, and I suck back tears. Part of me

wants to unleash it all on my sister, but that would be betraying Noah.

We get in the limo we rented for the day, along with my mom and Rylan.

"Hey, Ryguy, I heard you're walking down the aisle with Calista Bailey?" Chevelle loves to bait him about Dori's granddaughter.

"Not my idea," he deadpans.

"They also have a soccer tournament tomorrow. Rylan is going to drive them and there are supposed to be some scouts there," Mom says.

"You guys are playing together?" I ask.

"Not enough girls, so we had to do a mixed team this year." Rylan stares out the window.

"It's okay to like her," Posey says.

Rylan rolls his eyes. "Why don't we talk about how Mandi might be pregnant?"

All eyes fall to my stomach.

"What?" I ask.

"Everyone's concerned this wedding isn't real, but no one's considered you might be pregnant. I figure you'll try to pretend it's a honeymoon baby." Rylan's smug expression says this is payback for all the times we've given him hell over Calista.

"There's no baby, and who doesn't think this wedding is real?" I look around and each of my sisters and my mother dip their heads. Oh god, I don't know what to do. Do I just tell them the truth?

"It was all so fast, we couldn't make sense of it at first. But we see the way you love Noah now." My mom smiles.

"And I have to hear how much you guys love each other every night." Chevelle points at Rylan. "The pregnancy thing could be true. They're like rabbits, you guys, I swear."

"Chevelle!" I screech.

"What? It's true. Multiple times a night? You guys really can't keep your hands off one another. But it's beautiful. Just saying." She smiles while Rylan looks horrified. When he looks present again, she says to him, "It's not all that great. Don't go trying it until you love someone, okay?"

"God, stop," Rylan says, covering his ears. "I hate being the youngest in this family."

We arrive at the inn, which I'm sure Rylan is thankful for. He's out of the car before it's barely come to a full stop.

We're hurried up to a room set aside for me, and I'm hyperaware that Noah is in this building somewhere. It's as if I can feel his presence.

I change into my dress, and the girls change into theirs. Dori arrives with Calista, who is wearing a beautiful navy dress that shows off how much she's grown over the years. Her dark hair is twisted into an updo with little rhinestones in it. She's shy and quiet and eventually disappears downstairs.

Emelia arrives wearing her white flower girl dress, and my mom hands her the basket of flowers.

Before I have time to process it all, it's time to walk down the aisle. I cover my stomach with my hand, trying to calm my nerves.

"Come on, Mandi, you can do this," I say to myself. My chest is tight, and my heart is racing.

We all head downstairs, and I assume Noah must already be outside with the preacher who is marrying us. Hank waits for me at the bottom of the stairs, and I swear there are tears in his eyes.

"Now's the time if you want to run." He signals toward the door with a nod.

I laugh. "No. I'm good."

Kind of.

Not really.

He gives me his arm. "Then let's get you married."

We head over to the patio entrance we'll be walking out of and stand at the back of the bridal party line. All my sisters smile back at me, and Logan holds little Noah, who has a pillow the grandmas made with fake rings tied to it. I can't see much through the windows. Whoever took up decorating the area made the balcony overlooking the bay look perfect though.

The bridal music plays, and finally Hank steps forward. "I just want you to know how honored I am that you asked me to walk you down the aisle. All I want is your happiness." He kisses my cheek and lowers my veil over my face.

I bite back the tears building in my eyes. I don't know if it's emotion or panic or both, but I feel about a second away from losing it. We step out and I look down the aisle, needing to see Noah, to remind myself why I'm doing this.

My mouth drops open when I see Noah standing under an arbor that looks the same as a picture I tore out of a magazine when I was younger.

"What is that?" I whisper.

"It's an arbor for you," Hank says. "From Noah and me."

I soak in every little piece of it. The detailed carving, which I know was all Hank. The flowers just like in the picture.

"Noah?" I ask.

"He can tell you himself. First, we need to get you down the aisle."

Every step down the aisle, I take in Noah, standing so tall and handsome in a suit rather than a tuxedo. His hands are clasped in front of him, and he looks more distinguished than I've ever seen him. His smile is so welcoming and warm, and that should bring me happiness, but I only feel sorrow because I know he doesn't feel the same way that I do about him.

I reach the end of the aisle and Hank lifts my veil, kisses my cheek, and shakes hands with Noah. Noah's hand lands in mine as he takes me the last few steps under the arbor.

"It's beautiful," I say.

"You're beautiful. You're stunning." His gaze soaks me in.

"Thank you." I feel the blush set in as the preacher asks everyone to sit.

I look up at the arbor again and think about everything it signifies. The preacher is talking about love and loyalty, cherishing the person you love. Noah squeezes my hands and I look up, tears in my eyes.

"Are you okay?" Noah whispers.

I feel as though I can't get enough air. My chest gets tighter and it's all I can do to stand in place. I shake my head and look at the preacher. "I need to stop you."

He abruptly cuts off what he was saying.

I look at Noah. "I'm sorry, I can't marry you."

He exhales, and I swear even the seagulls stop squawking to listen in on our conversation.

"I have to choose me."

His eyes widen.

"You're a wonderful man, Noah. So much so that I fell in love with you. And as much as I want to marry you, I can't. Because I deserve a man who loves me too. A wedding where we're both equally invested in our future—together. I wanted the arbor so badly because I thought it signified the love and bond a couple getting married share, but this one doesn't. I'm worthy of having a great love in my life. I'm sorry that you can't be it."

He says nothing as the first tear falls down my cheek. I look out at the crowd and back at him.

"I'm so sorry I can't go through with it, but please know, I'm choosing to break my heart now, rather than in a year. I was right there with you until I stepped out and saw the arbor. It reminded me of a little girl who had hopes of finding her one true love. The man who would stand by her side and love her unconditionally. The man who loved her back."

I rise on my tiptoes and place a quick kiss on his lips, knowing it will be the last time.

Then I slide the engagement ring off my finger and return it to him before I rush back down the aisle, whispering sorry to everyone I pass.

I'll always look back on my time with Noah with love, but I need to choose myself this time around. The irony is that Noah is the one who taught me that lesson.

Noah

Mandi's mom, Hank, and all her sisters run after her.

I stand at the end of the aisle, unsure what to tell everyone who's left, so I opt for the simple truth. "There's no wedding. Thank you all for coming."

I step away from the arbor and rush down the aisle, my heart feeling as if it's been carved out of my chest.

"Noah!" My mom follows me into the parking lot. "Noah!"

I have nowhere to go at this point. Mandi couldn't be more right. She does deserve better, and I already knew that when she agreed to be my fake fiancée.

"What's going on? What did she mean? You don't love her?" Grandma is right behind my mom, and my dad trails behind them.

Seeing them all together—the cause for all this, besides my own stupidity—is like a hot coal burning in my chest where my heart used to be.

I run a hand through my hair and pull on the back of my neck. "It was all fake."

"What was?" Mom says in a gentle tone, obviously seeing my emotions but not understanding.

"The engagement, the wedding. I'm so sick of being in

the middle of you guys!" I throw up my arms and look between my dad and grandma. "Being torn apart like two kids tugging on a stuffed animal."

"It's not real?" Grandma's hand is on her chest, and I have a brief worry that maybe this won't be good for her heart, something I hadn't considered until now.

"When I told you I was engaged at the hospital, Mandi didn't know anything about it. I lied to you all with the hopes it would get the two of you to mend your differences. Then I made a deal with Mandi that if she married me, I'd help her out with the inn. She agreed." God, it all sounds so moronic when I say it out loud.

"I don't believe it. I just can't believe it. You two are just so..." My mom shakes her head. "I see it between you two, Noah. There's love there."

My chest tightens. "A love that can never grow. We live two very different lives. Her life is here, and mine is out there." I gesture toward the mountains in the distance.

"You did all this so I would talk to your grandma again?" My dad looks at Grandma, his eyes narrowed. "Look what you've done! You've pulled this poor Greene family into our drama."

Grandma holds up her hands. "This isn't my fault, this is yours."

"Mine?" my dad shouts.

"We should take this somewhere else," my mom says to my dad, glancing around the parking lot.

"How could you selling my father's company, our family company, out from under me be my fault? You left me and my family desolate. How could that be my fault?"

"Because I had other plans," Grandma says with heat in her voice.

"Plans that left my family without the security of my job.

I had to go searching and couldn't pay for Noah's college. And—"

"And you found happiness in the end, didn't you? You didn't want to work for that company for the rest of your life. We both know it. You were going to do so because you'd heard your father talk about how important it was to pass down the family business, so you felt you had to. And if you took it over, so would have Noah. I watched your father turn into a shell of who he was while we were married, and it was all because of that company. I wasn't going to allow it to happen to either of you. I begged him to sell well before you'd ever taken over, Rex. But he wouldn't do it, so I did it when he died, and I regret nothing."

My dad looks at my mom and shakes his head as though he doesn't understand.

"Then why not just share the money with us? At least enough to get by. Mom, you left us with nothing." I hear the pain in Dad's voice.

Grandma's face softens a bit. "Not my finest moment, I'll agree. I shouldn't have taken everything, but I didn't want to give you a portion of the profit because you would've settled. There's this picture that you painted for me your junior year in art class." She smiles. "It's a beautiful landscape. You'd gone out to that mountain range every weekend for a month to make sure you had it correct. Such devotion to the art. It hangs in my bedroom now to remind me that although you hate me, at least you're happy. That's all a mother really wants for her child. You never would've pursued art if I hadn't sold that company."

My dad remains quiet.

She looks at me. "And you, you'd never be a photographer because you would've been miserable and preparing to take over for your dad someday. Why do you think your grandfather turned into a drunk? He hated that company." She shakes her head and looks down as if she's remembering something particular.

"Midge, why didn't you just tell us?" Mom asks.

"Because it wouldn't have happened otherwise. I saw no other way. If I'd promised you the money, you'd just be waiting around for me to hand it over. This way, you had to find a way to make what you loved work."

"And you let yourself be collateral damage?" Mom gives her a hug, puts her arm around Grandma's shoulders, and turns to my dad. "She's right. That business was sucking the life out of you. I'd see the stress when you'd come home late at night, and it was clear how much you didn't want to go to work each morning. You're so much happier painting."

"Now that I can make a living at it," he grumbles.

"I should've given you some to get by at least. I apologize for that." Grandma takes off her glasses and wipes her eyes. "I was just so upset by your reaction. You get your stubbornness from me, not your father, in case you haven't guessed."

"Oh, Mom." Dad shakes his head and grips the back of his neck.

Grandma digs into her purse and pulls out two envelopes. "Here you go." She hands one to Dad and another to me. "Now we're square. This is your profit from the sale, plus some extra because I had it invested all these years."

Neither of us opens the envelopes. My dad shoves his in his jacket pocket, then he steps forward and hugs my grandma.

I'm happy to see them put the past behind them. That was the goal, right? Then why don't I feel as elated as I should? I look at the inn, wondering if Mandi is watching and wishing she was next to me, smiling up at me with happiness that they've come together again.

Then all three turn to me.

"Now you, Noah." Mom's eyes are no longer teary; they're filled with fire. "What were you thinking? You obviously hurt her."

"I don't want to talk about it," I say and head toward my truck.

"Stop running away," my dad shouts.

"I'm not running. She ran out on the wedding." I don't stop or turn my head when I speak.

"Because it was fake!" Midge yells.

It didn't feel very fake when I was up there. But I know my grandma is right.

I stop and turn to face them. "I'm not sure what you want me to do?"

Mom steps forward. "Can you really look me in the eye and tell me that you don't love that girl?"

My jaw clenches. "Love isn't enough. Grandma gave up a relationship with you for over ten years to make sure you were happy. Mandi and I want different things out of life."

"Sometimes you sacrifice for the ones you love." Grandma puts her hand on my arm. "I know she's the one for you. I know that you love her."

I get my keys out of the pocket of my suit jacket and unlock my truck. "Do me a favor and get my things from her house? I'm leaving for a job in a few days. I'll be at Glacier Point Resort if you need me."

I climb in my truck and get as far away from the inn as I can before I go running to Mandi, making her promises I can't make good on.

Two weeks later...

The weather is hot, and I'm camped out on the sand with my camera on a tripod, snapping pictures of the surfer who's about to win.

Being in Southern California has been a great distraction, but Mandi is always there in the back of my head. I haven't reached out to her because it wouldn't be fair. She said what she had to at the altar. What am I going to do—argue that she's wrong when I know she's right? What would be the point?

Willy, another photographer who has been alongside me the past few days, comes over. "Want to get a drink tonight?"

"Sure."

"Good, I have a few friends to keep us busy." He looks back where he came from, and I turn to see two girls in skimpy bikinis waving at us. "It can be isolating being a freelance photographer."

I look again at the girls and then at him.

He pats me on the back. "I'll see you in a bit." He disappears with his camera in his hands.

Maybe if I put myself out there, I'll get Mandi out of my system. Then again, the last time I thought I'd get her out of my system, all I did was have sex with her over and over. It never worked. And going out with those girls isn't going to work either.

"Be careful with Willy," Nate says, positioning his camera next to mine. "Did you know he's married?"

"Seriously? That's fucked up."

Nate shows me his own wedding ring. "Anyway, trouble

always finds him, especially in the surf circuit. I don't know how the guy gets more action than the surfers."

I chuckle. "Because the girls think they can get closer to the surfers through him?" I raise my eyebrows.

Nate laughs. "You're not new at this, are you?"

"Nope. Usually do wildlife but took this gig to get out of town."

I hate to admit it, but I searched for any job that would get me out of Sunrise Bay after the wedding. I knew the lines were blurring between Mandi and me, and if I stuck it out there, I couldn't predict what would happen. Mandi needed to know that things were still going to happen the way we said they were. That I'd leave and be gone for most of the year.

"You skipping bail or something?"

I laugh. "No. Just personal reasons." I look at his sparkling ring as he snaps a picture. "Can I ask you a question?"

He shrugs. "Sure."

"How on earth do you make your marriage work?"

He looks at his ring and laughs. "Well, it's not as simple as I'm going to tell you, but there's a lot of phone sex. There's me turning down jobs. Her coming with me when she can. It's like every marriage, I guess—compromise."

I look through the viewfinder and snap off a shot. "Were you a photographer before you got married?"

He nods. "Traveled the world. Met her on her first trip to Europe. Before kids, she came with me a lot more, but now the kids need stability."

"You could do something that leaves you at home?"

"I'd resent her for it and we both know it. We're a special breed. And it's probably selfish of me, but I wasn't gonna give up either one of my loves. Don't tell her, but she comes first. Always." He doesn't say anything for a minute. "I take it that's why you ran? A woman?"

I nod because Nate will probably get it more than anyone else.

"Well, if she loves you and you love her, you'll get through it. She'll understand your need for adventure, and you'll appreciate her that much more while you're gone. But there are times when I get asked to do an assignment and she'll look at me and I know she needs me there. So I turn it down and stay home."

I look at him. "And you don't get mad?"

"I'm never mad when I have to spend time with my wife. You really have to make the decision yourself. Oh shit, check that out." He runs over to where the winning surfer is being carried on the shoulders of his supporters.

They lower him to the sand, and he disregards everyone but the woman pushing through the crowd to get to him. When she reaches him, he takes her head in his hands and she's smiling wide like Mandi always did for me. They kiss while the crowd is still going crazy for the guy. I don't follow surfing, but I know they're gone a lot during the year. If all these people are able to make relationships work while they travel, why can't Mandi and I?

Jesus, am I this much of a fucking idiot?

Spoiler alert: yes.

I take my camera off the stand and pack up my stuff.

On my way off the beach, Willy stops me. "So, we're all set for tonight."

"Sorry, man, I gotta go."

His mouth drops open. "Where? What do I tell them?"

"Tell them I'm taken." I turn around. "And tell them you are too."

Chapter Twenty-eight

Mandi

I'm walking downtown, past the makeshift studio that Noah had used. It's been cleaned out and there's a for rent sign in the window. Just the sight of it makes my stomach lurch, but I keep my chin up and keep walking.

My family was surprised and disappointed when I confessed to them why I'd had to walk out of the wedding. Although they were skeptical about our relationship, they all said they'd seen the love between us as the weeks went on.

Nikki's exact words were, "He put up with baby Noah being a brat to him, so I thought he was a keeper."

Chevelle's, "I saw it, Mandi. The man loves you."

And maybe that's true, but it wasn't meant to be.

Last I heard, he moved all his stuff to his parents' place, since his house in Greywall is currently being rented, and flew out to California for that surf contest photo shoot.

I pick up a coffee at The Grind and walk over to the inn. With the changes Noah and I made, I've been changing up the clientele I'm focusing on and offering special packages paired with different businesses in town. I'm marketing the inn as the perfect romantic getaway for anyone looking to escape their ordinary lives, and it seems to be working.

Theo and I have a package where they stay and learn glass blowing and pottery at his store.

I have one with Truth or Dare Brewery, where guests get a meal and a flight of beer included.

Two Brothers and an Egg suggested a picnic lunch at the bay with their stay.

In the short time I've been promoting the packages, they've been successful. Seems lots of people are looking for a place to come and relax and remember why they fell in love with each other.

The arbor from our wedding, although painful to look at, remains on the balcony for any couples to use if they want to use the inn as a place to get married, although I haven't booked any weddings yet.

Trina is behind the desk when I arrive, and I give her a smile as I make my way over to reception.

"Thanks for opening up."

"You're welcome," she says and grabs her bag. "Francois is having another fit about the dinner."

"Okay, I'll go check it out." I put my overnight bag behind the desk, not wanting to go upstairs to the room right away.

Trina's hand runs down my arm. "You're looking good."

I laugh. "You mean not as depressed as I have been?"

She tilts her head and gives me a sad smile. "I just meant you look good. You're too good for him."

"Well, I'm not sure about that. Relationships fail all the time. Sometimes it's not really anyone's fault."

I don't blame Noah. Not at all. He was who he was when I met him, and that's the man I fell for. I just wish he could have loved me enough to give an inch on his lifestyle. I wish he desired me as much as he desires a life full of adventure and travel. But he doesn't, so it is what it is.

"Amanda!" Francois calls from the dining room.

"Have a great night." I put the bell on the counter and head into the kitchen. "Can we not shout in front of the guests please?"

He has the fridge open and is staring inside. "You people cannot keep eating all the ingredients and not telling me. I have no ice cream."

I bite my lip because that was me. "Sorry, I'll get you some more."

"You tell the guest." He throws his hands in the air.

"Fine, I will." I roll my eyes and turn to leave.

"And Amanda?"

I stop and turn around.

"You're looking better."

"Thank you." I hate that everyone has to comment about my appearance.

I'm making my way over to the table in question when Cam comes up to me in the middle of the dining room. "Who is this guy?"

My forehead wrinkles. "I'm sorry?"

"Chevelle is dating some guy named Derek. Who is he? What do you know about him?"

I shrug. "I don't know. He said he was working at the docks."

His eyes narrow. "I haven't heard of him," Cam says, nostrils flaring.

"Just relax, she can handle herself." I run my hand down his arm.

He blows out a breath. "Your brothers need to keep a better eye on her."

"Okay, I'll tell them." I slide past him. "Now excuse me."

I go to the table to apologize for the lack of ice cream and suggest one of our pies.

Between the inn and the restaurant, I savor the silence once the restaurant is shut down. I'm sitting at the computer, playing solitaire, when rain pelts the windows. I check the reservation book, and damn it, Trina took a late reservation without a phone number again.

I start another game as headlights shine through the window. I can't deny that déjà vu causes my stomach to fill with butterflies. The door opens and I bite my bottom lip, wondering if...

"Sorry I'm late," the man steps in. A man who isn't Noah.

I stand. "It's okay. I assume you're..." I look at the book. "George?"

"That's me. The jobsite took too long and I'm meeting my wife here tomorrow."

"Well, we're happy to have you at SunBay Inn." I start the check-in process and get him assigned to the last room available, sliding the key over to him. "Just up the stairs to your left."

"Is the kitchen open?" he asks.

"I'm sorry, it's not. But we'll start serving breakfast at six." I dig into the cabinet behind me and hand him a bag of snacks I have for the latecomers who arrive after the dining room is closed. I had the idea after Noah came in so late the night we met. "Here are a few things to tide you over. Some chips, granola bars, and a water."

He lifts the bag. "Thanks."

He goes upstairs and I turn off the computer, then round the desk to lock the door and put up the closed sign. But the door opens just before I reach it. I step back, startled by the large body in the doorway. He steps in, pushing back the gray hood of the rain jacket.

My stomach ignites like the baby butterflies are just learning to fly. Noah.

"Hi," I say.

"Hi. I was wondering if you have a room available?"

I close my eyes for a moment at the sound of his deep voice. "Um... no. I'm sorry I just rented out the last room." I stare at him, cataloging the differences since the last time I saw him. Not much is different except his cheeks are a little sunburned and he has dark circles under his eyes.

"I should've called."

We stand there, staring at each other.

"Not even a broom closet or anything, huh?"

I shake my head. "What brings you to SunBay Inn?"

"A woman."

I fight the smile that wants to form on my face. "Oh really?"

He nods once. "I need to grovel."

"What did you do that was so awful?"

"I was a stupid, stupid man and it took me way too long to realize that I can't be without her." He takes one step closer to me.

My breath hitches. "And now? What changed your mind?"

"I realized what an idiot I was. And how scared I was that we couldn't make it work, so I let it overshadow what we could have together if it did. I'll do just about anything to keep her in my life."

One corner of my lips lifts. "I'm sure she'll accept your apology. I mean, you're pretty easy on the eyes."

"You think so?" He looks me up and down. "She's a knockout, so I'm not sure I measure up. She could have her pick of any man."

"I'm sure you measure up just fine. You know, I do have one room available, but you'd have to share a bed with the owner."

"What do you think the woman I love will think about that?"

I lick my bottom lip. "I think she'll understand. I mean, we can't send you back out in the rain. And she really loves you too."

"She does? Nothing changed during the weeks I was lost?" He steps toward me, caging me in against the reservation desk.

"No. She is still very much in love with you."

"I'm sorry, Mandi. I was so stupid." He runs his hand over my hair. "I don't care what we have to do. I want this to work because you not being in my life isn't an option."

"Good, because not having you in my life doesn't work for me either." I rise to my tiptoes, and he grabs my head, bending down and capturing my mouth in a kiss that makes my knees weak.

He closes the kiss and rests his forehead against mine. "Tell me the kitchen is open?"

I laugh. "Only for you."

"This time around, can I request room service?"

I smile. "Sure. I hope you're a good tipper."

"Oh, believe me, I'm a great tipper." He bends down to my ear. "In sexual favors."

"Then let's go." I tug him by the arm toward the kitchen.

He shrugs off his wet jacket and hangs it on the coat hook, then catches up to me on the way to the kitchen. His arms wrap around my waist, and he pulls me against him. Through the window is the arbor, and I think we both stare at it for a moment, wet and shining in the patio lights.

"Mandi?"

I turn around and he lowers to the floor, the ring I gave him back nestled in a ring box. "Will you marry me?"

My hands fly to my mouth. "What? Why?"

"Because I've fallen madly in love with you."

"As simple as that, huh?"

He smiles. "As simple as that."

"Yes, I will marry you. For real this time."

He slides the ring back onto my finger, and it feels as if he's giving me back a piece of my soul. I join him on my knees and kiss him again.

"Truth?" he asks.

"Yeah."

"I think I fell in love with you the first time I saw you."

I cup his bearded cheek. "Me too."

We kiss again. And ditch the kitchen for my room at the inn.

Epilogue

Mandi

A week later...

I'm dressed once again in my wedding gown, my sisters are in their dresses from the sewing circle, and we're walking down the stairs just as we did last time. Except this time I'm getting married for real.

Hank waits for me at the bottom of the stairs and offers me his arm.

Since this is the real deal this time around, I called my dad to let him know I was getting married, but he couldn't make it here on such short notice. I was less disappointed than a daughter probably should be. But I honestly don't feel like I'm missing anything when I look at Hank's smiling face while he waits for me.

It's literally like someone pressed rewind on the entire last three weeks, except this time there's no debate in my head. I'm completely at peace with what I'm about to do.

Neither Noah nor I thought we should waste any more time just being engaged. And I really wanted to be the first one married under that arbor. So, we planned this wedding with a very small guest list and scheduled it on a weekday.

I walk out to the balcony that overlooks the bay and see

the rows of white chairs and one gorgeous man at the end of the aisle, waiting for me under the arbor.

When Noah looks at me, his smile is everything. I never dreamed about what the man I would marry would look like. All I know is that he possessed everything Noah does. He's kind and generous and loves me for me. He desires me, craves me, and constantly tells me how much I mean to him. I'm not sure I ever really thought I could find a man like him.

We walk up the aisle, and Hank puts his hand on mine to slow me down a bit because this time I'm eager to reach my groom. Eager to have his hands in mine. Eager to become Mrs. Noah Winters.

What feels like a lifetime later, we reach the end of the aisle. Hank lifts my veil, kisses my cheek, and hands me over to Noah. Noah takes my hands and holds them tightly.

"You look stunning... again."

I grin. "You look handsome... again."

We both laugh and the preacher stops speaking for a moment.

"Sorry," we mumble and look at each other, trying not to laugh again.

This time, I listen to the words the preacher says about how we need to love and cherish each other. Then we say our vows, exchange rings, and are announced as "Mr. and Mrs. Noah and Amanda Winters."

And then the best part. Noah's warm hands on my cheeks. My head tilts to look up as he bends down to kiss his bride. His kiss, as always, comes with promises, and this one tells me he's going to love me all of my life.

We walk down the aisle, and at the end, he lifts me off my feet, twirling me around. When he kisses me again, his tongue parts my lips, silently telling me to just wait for tonight.

Of course, we're not staying at the inn. I'm giving my team another chance to show off how they can manage without me, because we're leaving on a surprise honeymoon. Noah refuses to tell me where we're going but gave me a list of five things to bring. A bikini, flip-flops, a casual dress, lingerie, and my favorite sex toy.

"Mrs. Winters," he says and stares at me, "I love you."

"I love you."

Our brief moment of privacy gets interrupted by my big family and Noah's smaller one offering their congratulations. Even baby Noah gives Noah a high five, but still says he's not Noah, to which everyone laughs.

"Time to eat!" Francois announces.

Everyone shuffles into the dining room. I closed it for anyone other than wedding guests.

I stop Chevelle when she and Derek start toward the exit of the dining room. "Where are you going?"

"I'm just saying goodbye to Derek. He has to get to work," she says.

"Not sure who plans a wedding during the week," Derek grumbles.

"Stop it," Chevelle says. "How about a thank you?"

Derek doesn't say anything in response to Chevelle. "Congratulations," he says to me.

It's all I can do to not lay into this guy. But I won't make a scene at my wedding, so instead I say, "Thanks. Sorry you can't stay." Not.

"I'll be right back," Chevelle says and squeezes my hand.

I turn and find Noah waiting for me, so I walk right into his arms.

"What's that about?" He looks over my head at where my sister and her douchebag boyfriend are departing.

"Derek has to go to work. Too bad."

"Definitely not going to be missed. What does Chevelle see in that guy? He can't even do polite conversation." Noah puts his fingers under my chin and tilts my head up, then kisses me chastely.

"I'm not sure," I say. "Come on, we have guests."

We go inside where everyone is clinking their glasses and shouting, "Kiss, kiss, kiss."

Noah dips me and kisses me again, not that I'm complaining. If I had my way, we'd be on our mysterious honeymoon already.

The door opens from the outside and I spot Chevelle sliding in and heading straight to the bathroom. But Cam is standing right at the entry to the hallway that leads to the restrooms. I can't take my eyes off of what's going on behind everyone's backs.

Cam inches close to Chevelle, touches her eyes, and his face turns to stone. He asks her something, and she shakes her head. Their conversation is definitely heated. Cam walks past her and out the door. Chevelle follows.

What the hell?

"Excuse me," I say and weave through the tables, thanking people quickly as they give their congratulations again. I reach Chevelle right before she's about to go through the inn door. "Chevelle?"

I reach for her arm, and she stops but keeps her face tipped down away from me. I take her chin in my finger and thumb and turn her toward me. My stomach drops. Her eye is swollen and red and definitely on its way to becoming a black eye.

Now I understand completely why Cameron had such a murderous expression. The question is—what is he going to do about it?

TheEnd

ALSO BY PIPER RAYNE

The Baileys

Lessons from a One-Night Stand (FREE)

Advice from a Jilted Bride

Birth of a Baby Daddy

Operation Bailey Wedding (Novella)

Falling for My Brother's Best Friend

Demise of a Self-Centered Playboy

Confessions of a Naughty Nanny

Operation Bailey Babies (Novella)

Secrets of the World's Worst Matchmaker

Winning my Best Friend's Girl

Rules for Dating Your Ex

Operation Bailey Birthday (Novella)

The Greene Family

My Twist of Fortune (Free Prequel)

My Beautiful Neighbor (FREE)

My Almost Ex

My Vegas Groom

A Greene Family Summer Bash (Novella)

My Sister's Flirty Friend

My Unexpected Surprise

My Famous Frenemy

A Greene Family Vacation (Novella)

My Scorned Best Friend

My Fake Fiancé

My Brother's Forbidden Friend

A Greene Family Christmas (Novella)

Lake Starlight

The Problem with Second Chances

The Issue with Bad Boy Roommates

The Trouble with Runaway Brides

The Drawback of Single Dads

Plain Daisy Ranch

One Last Summer

The One I Left Behind

The One I Stood Beside

The One I Didn't See Coming

Modern Love

Charmed by the Bartender

Hooked by the Boxer

Mad about the Banker

Single Dads Club

Real Deal

Dirty Talker

Sexy Beast

Hollywood Hearts

Mister Mom

Animal Attraction

Domestic Bliss

Bedroom Games

Cold as Ice

On Thin Ice

Break the Ice

Chicago Law

Smitten with the Best Man

Tempted by my Ex-Husband

Seduced by my Ex's Divorce Attorney

Blue Collar Brothers

Flirting with Fire

Crushing on the Cop

Engaged to the EMT

White Collar Brothers

Sexy Filthy Boss

Dirty Flirty Enemy

Wild Steamy Hook-up

The Rooftop Crew

My Bestie's Ex

A Royal Mistake

The Rival Roomies

Our Star-Crossed Kiss

The Do-Over

A Co-Workers Crush

Hockey Hotties

Countdown to a Kiss (Free Prequel)

My Lucky #13 (FREE)

The Trouble with #9

Faking it with #41

Tropical Hat Trick (Novella)

Sneaking around with #34

Second Shot with #76

Offside with #55

Kingsmen Football Stars

False Start (Free Prequel)

You Had Your Chance, Lee Burrows

You Can't Kiss the Nanny, Brady Banks

Over My Brother's Dead Body, Chase Andrews

Chicago Grizzlies

On the Defense (Free Prequel)

Something like Hate

Something like Lust

Something like Love

The Nest

Mr. Heartbreaker

Mr. Broody

Mr. S (Title to be revealed)

Mr. C (Title to be revealed)

Holiday Romances

Single and Ready to Jingle

Claus and Effect

Merry Kissmas

Cockamamie Unicorn Ramblings

Many of you might not know, but we usually have all our cover photos for a series before we even start writing book one. So the minute we saw Wander's photo for this cover, we were sold. We already knew we wanted to have a plus size heroine but finding a custom picture of a curvy woman is HARD! So, the minute he released the photo to us, Mandi was born in our minds. And holy hotness, so was Noah.

Funny thing is we usually name all our heroes and heroines beforehand as well, so we had Mandi down as having a guy named Noah as her hero. But then as the kids are born throughout a series, we usually fly by the seat of our pants in naming them. So, Nikki's baby was named Noah, and somewhere between writing and editing the bonus scene of My Unexpected Surprise, our photographer Noah was written in so we couldn't change our hero Noah's name. So rather than stressing about it, we decided to have fun with it! We hope you enjoyed Nikki's banter and baby Noah's outrage at not being the only Noah in the world. LOL These things happen. Rayne can attest to this as her sister-in-law married someone with the same name as Rayne's husband.

We know a lot of you were wondering how many grandkids Midge had an were hoping we might venture into Greywall to tell her grandkids story. But don't fret! It doesn't mean that we won't venture into Greywall to find another big family someday, but since we're moving on to the younger generation in Lake Starlight after The Greene Family series is complete we didn't want to corner ourselves in.

As always, we have a lot of people to thank for getting this book into your hands...

Nina and the entire Valentine PR team.
Cassie from Joy Editing for line edits.
Ellie from My Brother's Editor for line edits.
Rosa from My Brother's Editor for proofreading.
Hang Le for the cover and branding for the entire series.
Wander Aguiar for his awesome job of giving us our muses Mandi and Noah.
Bloggers who consistently carve out time to read, review and/or promote us.
Piper Rayne Unicorns who give us a safe space online to chat!
Readers who took the time to read our story and champion this series to other readers. We are grateful beyond words for your support!
The final full length Greene book is next but no tears just yet. We've all been waiting on pins and needles for Chevelle and Cam to get their act together. We know their wounds, we feel their sexual tension, and it's time for all of it to come to a head. My Brother's Forbidden Friend is next!
xo,
Piper & Rayne

ABOUT PIPER & RAYNE

Piper Rayne is a USA Today Bestselling Author duo who write "heartwarming humor with a side of sizzle" about families, whether that be blood or found. They both have e-readers full of one-clickable books, they're married to husbands who drive them to drink, and they're both chauffeurs to their kids. Most of all, they love hot heroes and quirky heroines who make them laugh, and they hope you do, too!

9 798888 714195 4